Ans	_____	M.L.	
ASH	_____	MLW	_____
Bev	_____	Mt.Pl	_____
C.C.	_____	NLM	_____
C.P.	_____	Ott	_____
Dick	_____	PC	_____
DRZ	_____	PH	_____
ECH	_____	P.P.	_____
ECS	_____	Pion.P.	_____
Gar	_____	Q.A.	_____
GRM	_____	Riv	_____
GSP	_____	RPP	_____
G.V.	_____	Ross	_____
Har	_____	S.C.	_____
JPCP	_____	St.A.	_____
KEN	_____	St.J	_____
K.L.	_____	St.Joa	_____
K.M.	_____	St.M.	_____
L.H.	_____	Sgt	_____
LO	_____	T.H.	_____
Lyn	_____	TLLO	_____
L.V.	_06/09_	T.M.	_____
McC	_____	T.T.	_____
McG	_____	Ven	_____
McQ	_____	Vets	_____
MIL	_____	VP	_____
	_____	Wat	_____
	_____	Wed	_____
	_____	WIL	_____
	_____	W.L.	_____
	_____		
	_____		
	_____		

Louise Pakeman was born in Cannock but has lived in Australia since 1968. Now retired, she has worked in publishing and as a freelance journalist. Her previous novels are *Change of Skies*, *Flowers for the Journey*, and *A Pinch of Sugar*.

LOVE'S HERITAGE

In response to her mother's dying request, Maggie Townsend is on her way to England, with the address of a grandfather she barely knew existed. However, when Tim Fenton, a fellow Australian she meets on the journey, insists on giving her his contact details in London she begins to have qualms. Maggie finds that her relations are grander and stranger than she imagined. She is shocked when her grandfather refuses to acknowledge her, and by sinister undercurrents in the household. Tim and the aunt he is staying with prove to be true friends when events spiral out of control.

Books by Louise Pakeman
Published by The House of Ulverscroft:

THE PUMPKIN SHELL
CHANGE OF SKIES
FLOWERS FOR THE JOURNEY
A PINCH OF SUGAR

LOUISE PAKEMAN

LOVE'S HERITAGE

Complete and Unabridged

ULVERSCROFT
Leicester

First published in Great Britain in 2007 by
Robert Hale Limited
London

First Large Print Edition
published 2008
by arrangement with
Robert Hale Limited
London

British Library CIP Data

Pakeman, Louise, *1936 –*
  Love's heritage.—Large print ed.—
  Ulverscroft large print series: general fiction
  1. Australians—England—London—Fiction
  2. Grandparent and child—Fiction 3. Love stories
  4. Large type books
  I. Title
  823.9'2 [F]

  ISBN 978–1–84782–330–4

Published by
F. A. Thorpe (Publishing)
Anstey, Leicestershire

Set by Words & Graphics Ltd.
Anstey, Leicestershire
Printed and bound in Great Britain by
T. J. International Ltd., Padstow, Cornwall

This book is printed on acid-free paper

1

'It's OK, we're airborne!' The male voice in my ear sounded amused and just a little patronizing, so, without turning my head I replied as coolly as I could.

'I was not scared; just savouring the moment.'

I had noticed him, of course I had, though it was his hand baggage, camera and laptop computer that had caught my eye in the departure lounge causing me to label him 'tourist'.

'First time?' When I heard that irritating voice again I found my head swivelling of its own accord to take a look at the creature it emanated from. To my discomfiture I found myself staring straight into the most amazing navy-blue eyes. He was drop-dead gorgeous, and I couldn't imagine how my preoccupation with his gear had stopped me seeing him properly before.

'Yes.' To my embarrassment the single word came out midway between a squeak and a croak. I felt my cheeks grow warm and wished I had thought of an inspired lie. Somehow I didn't like the idea of him viewing me as young and naïve, overwhelmed by my first trip overseas, my first flight even.

I closed my eyes and sank back in my seat partly in an attempt to look blasé and partly so that I didn't have to look into those eyes. As we ascended my spirits soared with the Qantas jet. I let out a gusty sigh and with it came a sense of liberation as if I had left my problems down there on the tarmac. Little did I know that when the plane touched down at Heathrow I would pick up an even bigger load.

'Holiday?' He asked as the sounds of take-off subsided. He still sounded superior and I toyed with the idea of keeping my eyes closed and pretending to be asleep, but he spoke again.

'You can open your eyes now — I assure you we really are safely airborne.'

'I am visiting relatives,' I volunteered. I opened my eyes but looked out of the window as I answered his question.

'When you stay with rellies it can be a holiday — or not — it all depends . . . ' He tailed off, leaving the words 'on the relatives' floating between us. He still sounded faintly amused, maybe it was just part of the unique timbre of his voice, but at least I felt now that if he was laughing it was with me not at me. I relaxed.

'I don't know these particular relatives at all, so I have no idea whether or not it will turn out to be a holiday,' I confided, determined to enjoy myself whatever. 'But if it doesn't turn out any good then I shall just pack my bags and move on.'

'Good on you!' He nodded his approval. I felt a warm glow, then told myself that I didn't need his, or anyone else's approval. I was on my own now and only had myself to please. I shouldn't have thought that, it reminded me just why I was on the plane at all.

'What about you?'

'Partly work, partly pleasure,' he told me. 'I have an assignment to do then I am free to holiday, but I shall do a bit of freelance work and hope to extend my stay.'

'Oh,' I said, then because curiosity had always been my besetting vice, 'What do you do? What is your assignment? Anything to do with that expensive camera and what I guess is a computer?'

He laughed. 'Full marks for deduction! I'm a photo-journalist, mostly freelance. And how did you know my camera was expensive, you haven't seen it out of its case?'

'Photography is my thing,' I told him.

'Is that what you do for a living?'

'Yes,' I began, and then honesty compelled

me to admit that it was what I would *like* to do for a living. 'I did a course at our local TAFE College,' I told him, wishing I didn't sound so defensive. 'And I had a job photographing kids with Santa at our local shopping mall. Of course, Christmas put an end to that.' I fell silent remembering with a wrench the main reason why I had done nothing else. It was at Christmas that Mum had told me she was putting the antique shop on the market. I relived the shock her words had caused me. They had made me really look at her and notice how tired she looked, tired and suddenly much older.

'You mean SELL?' I'd asked, my voice strident with a nameless fear. I knew that my mother would not even consider such a course unless she was under enormous pressure. What happened next rocked my world. My tough, courageous and, I really believed, invincible mother, burst into tears.

'Oh, Maggie — Maggie dear!' She fished out a hanky and blew her nose and managed the shakiest of smiles. 'I hadn't meant to tell you — not yet anyway. But, well — I just have to. For one thing it isn't making money any more and . . . ' Her voice sort of died away on a sob and she looked away.

'And?' I prompted remorselessly. 'What else?' The words died in my throat as I looked

4

at her and knew the answer with a terrible certainty. 'You're sick, aren't you?' It was a statement really, not a question. As I said it, so many things I had noticed but ignored crowded my mind. Her days of utter exhaustion when she was either late opening her shop or didn't open at all. The fact that she almost never went to sales these days. Oh, there had been so many clues I had chosen to overlook.

She screwed her hanky into a ball and mumbled those terrible words: 'I'm not going to get better, darling.'

So the next few weeks had been spent, not working, or even looking for work, but in helping Mum sell the shop and caring for her as best I could till she went into hospital for the last time.

She left me with a letter to take to England for her family, my family too I supposed, and enough money to get me there and back, with a bit to spare.

I couldn't explain all this to a stranger, it was still too raw, so I just shifted in my seat, smiled brightly and turned my attention to the flight attendant pausing beside us with a trolley of goodies.

When we stopped at Singapore, Tim (by now we had exchanged names) seemed to take it as read that we would stay together. I was secretly thankful; without him I should in all probability have managed to lose myself, or forget everything browsing among the goods on display, but in his company I felt secure in one thing — he would get me back to that plane.

I tried not to let him see I was anything but cool, calm and sophisticated, but by the time we reached the last leg of the journey, my ever-active tongue had let me down. He'd had a run down of my life to date and knew I was quite alone in the world except for the unknown English relatives I was about to descend on.

'Are you being met?'

With the instruction to fasten our seat belts for landing, the enormity of my adventure had just hit me, my eyes were shut and I was waiting for the bump, I opened them again when I realized he was asking me a question.

'Um — sorry?' I grunted, his question honed into my not too happy thoughts and did nothing to reassure me.

'I asked if anyone was meeting you at the airport?'

I shook my head. 'No,' I mouthed over the increasing noise of landing. It was hardly likely, considering they were not, as yet, aware of my imminent arrival, or even, probably, of my existence. But I didn't tell Tim that.

Somehow I thought it would make me appear altogether too naïve and foolhardy in his eyes. I already looked that way to myself.

We soon bumped to a halt and I got my first look at England. It was much as I had expected, only more so; grey and rather forbidding. I shivered, but the chill came from within.

Tim, pulling our hand baggage down from the overhead rack, noticed. 'Hope you've brought warm clothes.' He appraised the jeans and shirt I was wearing as he handed down my light parka. He was putting on a warm fleece-lined thing over his sweater. 'England in February is a bit cooler than Australia.'

His words did nothing to raise my flagging spirits. Who but an idiot, I thought, would leave Australia in late summer for England in the grip of winter?

As I shuffled after him down the gangway of the plane he looked over his shoulder and said, 'Better stick with me.' It was a superfluous suggestion; only the fact that both my hands were full stopped me from actually hanging on to him physically.

As we made our way along endless walking platforms and struggled through all the dreary complexities of immigration and Customs, I wondered just what I would have done if fate, or a matchmaking flight attendant, hadn't put me next to Tim. Probably sat on a bench until I could get a seat on the next flight back to good old Oz, I reflected gloomily.

Tim had loaded all our cases on to one trolley so I had no choice but to follow it, and him. I found myself breaking into a trot now and then like a small child or a lost puppy.

'Where are we heading?' I asked rather breathlessly.

'Train.' His reply was economical and to the point.

'Oh.' My response was equally so.

He loaded our bags into a compartment, flopped down in a corner seat opposite me and gave me what I could only describe as a considering look. Considering — as in wondering what to do with me — rather than considerate. I turned away and looked out of the window.

'At least I can see you safely into London,' he said at last.

'You don't have to feel responsible for me,' I replied stiffly. It was humiliating to be seen as someone who needed looking after. But comforting as well.

'You're right — I don't. All the same . . . ' He tailed off and I went on looking determinedly out of the window, though God knows there wasn't much to see; just an endless stream of frazzled-looking travellers who did, however, at least seem to know what they were doing and where they were going.

'Tell me your plans.'

The question was so sudden and unexpected that I answered truthfully. 'I haven't any.'

'Where are you going then?'

'To my relations, like I told you.' I was defensive. After all, I did have some plans.

'Who live — where?' This was becoming an interrogation.

'Staffordshire,' I told him.

He was looking at me again in that considering way. I squirmed in my seat and resumed my observation of my fellow travellers boarding the train.

'Look, Maggie . . . ' he was leaning forward and the movement and the tone of his voice demanded my attention. 'I know it isn't really any business of mine — ' I nodded here to acknowledge the truth of that. 'But you do know what you are doing? I mean . . . ' He amended, 'are they expecting you?'

Another of my weaknesses beside curiosity has always been an inclination to be truthful. 'Well, no. Not exactly,' I admitted.

How could I tell him that not only were they not expecting me but that I was not at all sure of my welcome. Something of my thoughts must have shown in my face because he leaned even closer and to lend emphasis to his words reached across and touched me on the knee.

'Why don't you stay a day or so — or even the night — in London, then you can phone them? At least you can make sure they are at home before you set off into the blue.'

I had to admit it seemed like a good idea. 'Where could I stay?' I asked helplessly, again blowing my cover of sophisticated traveller.

Tim leaned back in his corner and smiled at me. 'With me.'

'With you!' Was I such a bad judge of character, such a greenhorn, that I had given myself into the care of a 'white slaver'? So ran my lurid thoughts.

He grinned at me, just as if he could read inside my head. 'Don't jump to conclusions, do I look sinister?'

I shook my head. 'Not really.' I managed a weak smile.

'What I was suggesting is that I take you along with me, I'm staying with my aunt out in Barnes. I'm sure she won't mind if I bring you along too.'

But I wasn't so sure; and it seemed either way I was going to land myself on the mercy of strangers. Slowly I shook my head. 'No, thanks all the same. I'll make my way to my relations and if anything goes wrong, well, I'll just book into a hotel for the night.'

He tried to dissuade me though I think he was secretly glad that he didn't have to turn up at his aunt's flat with a stray girl in tow.

By now our compartment had filled and the train was pulling away from the platform. He was still looking at me somewhat anxiously.

'Don't look at me like that,' I complained.

'Like what?' he parried, and I wished I had kept my mouth shut because now I had to reply.

'As if I am utterly helpless. I can assure you I am quite capable of looking after myself.' Fine words which, by the expression on his face, were not convincing.

He said nothing, just pulled his wallet out of his pocket, and drew out two business cards and a biro. He scribbled on one then passed them both to me. 'That's Penny's address and phone number,' he told me. 'If I'm not actually there she will know where I am. If things don't work out, or you need me, or — well — if you just want to get in touch . . . ' He tailed off then pointed to the other card. 'Write your address, the place you are going to, on there.'

I wanted to refuse and tell him he was

arrogant, bossy and chauvinistic, instead I meekly wrote down the address of my relatives and handed the card back to him.

'You haven't put their name,' was all he said as he scrutinized it. 'I don't know *your* surname either.'

'Mine is Townsend, my relatives are called Sinclair — they're my mother's family.' I turned over the card he had given me and looked at the printed side: Timothy Fenton, and a Melbourne address.

'Elwood Hall, Elwood,' he read aloud. 'Very grand!'

I ignored that; I could see that in true Aussie style he was not unduly impressed by a fine-sounding English address.

'How will you get there?' he asked now. 'Elwood I think is quite a way out of Stafford.' That was the least of my worries, I had to get to Stafford first. Once again he seemed to guess my thoughts. 'This train takes us into Paddington station, but trains for Stafford go from Euston.'

'Oh — well, I am sure I can get to the right train.' I must have looked doubtful for all my brave words, because he had that superior look again.

'Not to worry, I'll see you safely across London and on to the right train.'

'You must have been here before,' I

muttered rather ungraciously, unable to bring myself to express the gratitude I felt.

'This is about my fifth trip. In fact my aunt's place is as much home to me as anywhere else.'

I realized that though I had gabbled a lot about myself I really knew very little about him. I thought to remedy that during the rest of the train journey into London. However, Tim was not forthcoming, in fact the last thing he seemed to want to do was talk about himself, or anything else. He gave a great yawn, leaned back in his seat and closed his eyes.

'Jet lag,' he grumbled. 'I think it's catching up with me.'

The view of England sliding past the window, and my thoughts helped to keep me awake. I was, in fact, beginning to wonder if arriving unannounced on the doorstep of totally unknown relations was such a good idea after all.

True to his word Tim saw me safely across London and on to an express train for Stafford. He looked at his watch. 'With luck you may be there for a late lunch, or at least afternoon tea, it only takes a couple of hours to Stafford. I hope you can find your way to Elwood safely — there should be a bus.'

'I'll be fine,' I told him.

But when I came out of Stafford Station I opted for the easier alternative and joined the queue for taxis instead of humping my baggage across the road to try and locate a bus that would deliver me to my destination. The driver, whom I could only describe as taciturn, flung open the back passenger door for me and I clambered in and asked him to take me to Elwood.

'Whereabouts?' he asked, adding, 'It's about six miles, it won't be a cheap trip.'

'The Hall.' I told him shortly and, since conversation didn't seem to be the order of the day, settled back in my seat to take in the scenery.

After the wide streets of my home town in Country Victoria, Stafford seemed to me grey and congested, with narrow streets overfull of traffic and pavements overfull of people all hurrying and scurrying about their business, like so many ants. I, too, felt like an ant, but on the outside looking in.

I pulled myself up sharply realizing that I was just feeling homesick and giving into it would be no help. I was here — I was on the inside, whether I liked it or not, this was an adventure — a great adventure. As we drew away from the town and out through the suburbs, this idea began to take root and I felt a whole heap better, though I had to confess to something that felt very like the jitters. Natural curiosity and interest however took over as the taxi turned through large wrought-iron gates, and drew up outside a hefty-looking front door atop a flight of stone steps, flanked by two rather mild-looking stone lions.

As I hauled my cases out of the taxi on to the gravel drive and fumbled in my purse for the unfamiliar currency, I toyed with the idea of asking the driver to wait till I had gained admittance, or not, as the case may be. But while I debated with myself he pocketed the fare and drove off. Oh, well, if the worst came to the worst I would find some way out of here. My confidence flagged as I watched his tail lights disappear. Here I was in the middle of nowhere, standing in front of a somewhat forbidding house that showed no sign of life. I hoped his haste to be gone was not a bad omen as I toiled up the steps with my baggage.

Looking round for a bell to press I saw the chain at the side of the door and remembered my mother telling me about a small boy who had scandalized Ingram, the family butler, by asking him why there was a lavatory chain at the front door. Recalling this story I couldn't help but give a little giggle to myself as I tugged on the chain and heard an answering clamour reverberating through the house. The smile was still hovering on my lips so I kept it there when at last I heard the sound of what seemed to be a heavy bolt drawn back on the inside of the door. It slowly opened to reveal a very old man in a black coat now almost green with age, who, quite silently, just stood there, one hand on the partially opened door, looking at me.

I realized this must actually be Ingram, and managed to keep smiling even when he growled, 'If you are selling something you should have gone to the back door.'

'Wait!' I cried, desperation lending strength to my voice as I saw the door beginning to close inexorably in my face. I put my hand on it and backed my hunch, 'I'm not selling anything, Mr Ingram. My name is Maggie Townsend!'

The door didn't close, but it didn't open any more either. He leaned forward and peered at me through faded blue eyes behind steel-framed glasses, and slowly repeated my name with an air of bewilderment. I kept my hand firmly on the heavy door. 'My mother was Angela Sinclair,' I added quickly, guessing it would mean more to him than my own name.

He stepped forward so suddenly to peer into my face that I found myself stepping back. Fortunately the top step was very wide. He said after a scrutiny that left me feeling almost naked, 'You are like her. Yes, you are like her indeed.' Then he stepped back and opened the door wider and said. 'Well you'd best come in, I suppose.' He leaned forward and grabbed my largest case and pulled it inside. In spite of the reservation in his welcome I felt an instant liking for him and knew why my mother had always spoken of him with affection when she talked about her childhood. 'My Hilda anyway will be right glad to see you.' He smiled slightly now but it faded as he added in a sombre voice, 'I don't know about the family though — no, I can't promise a welcome there. I can't promise that at all.'

2

I humped my bags into the hallway and he closed the heavy door behind me. The sharp clang sounded very definite and somewhat chilling after his words of warning, but I smiled brightly in a determined effort to keep my flagging spirits high. I looked about me with interest as I stepped into my mother's old home, the place where she had been born and brought up and which therefore must, inevitably, be part of my own background and my make-up.

I was standing on a beautiful floor laid out in a geometrical pattern of coloured tiles including a sky-blue one that was most unusual. Footsteps on the wide curved staircase made me look up. An elderly woman with hair as white as the huge apron that enveloped her, came carefully down, her eyes on me. She paused an instant on the bottom step, with her hand on the polished banisters, looking from Mr Ingram to myself inquiringly, then moved closer, her expression puzzled, as she subjected me to a keen scrutiny. I saw her lips move slightly and barely heard her breathe: 'Miss Angie?'

The old man took hold of my elbow so that I had to move a step closer; it was almost as if he were presenting me to her, which in a way I suppose he was. 'No, my dear.' He shook his head slightly and there was a tremor in his voice. 'Not Miss Angie, but her daughter, Maggie.'

She stared at me in silence and feeling I had to put something into the void I said, as gently as I could, 'My mother is dead, Mrs Ingram.'

'Oh, Lord's sake!' she cried and, putting both hands under her apron, she flung it up over her head. I was fascinated, I had read in books of people doing this but had never seen anyone do it in real life. I looked to Mr Ingram anxiously.

'My Hilda thought a lot of your mother, she was her nanny, you know. She tends to get a bit muddled about time these days and when she saw you there, looking so like her, well, I suppose it sort of confused her.' He looked at me almost accusingly. 'You are very like her, you know!'

'So I'm told.'

Our little exchange however seemed to have enabled Hilda Ingram to move forward some twenty odd years in time and when she dropped the apron from her face she was quite composed and looked at me calmly as she repeated her husband's words. 'You are just like my poor Miss Angie, the very spit of her when she walked out of her home — for ever!'

I stifled a faint feeling of annoyance to hear my mother referred to as 'poor' along with the constant repetition of how like her I was. Not that I was ashamed of that but, well, I suppose everyone wants to be seen and accepted for themselves not for their likeness to someone else. However, the emotional moment seemed to have passed and the old lady was only brisk efficiency when she invited: 'Come along now into the kitchen and I'll make a pot of tea and you can talk to me.'

'The kitchen?' Her husband sounded doubtful. 'Don't you think — ?'

'No,' she cut in decisively, then turning to me said, 'Come along, my dear!'

I followed her meekly through an archway to the back and left of the hall, leaving my bags behind me. She led the way down a short dim passage; here the colourful tiles gave way to old-fashioned red and black quarries, and opened the door at the end.

The kitchen was what I had always imagined an English country kitchen would be. Light, warm, large and with an air of use, rather than actual shabbiness, that was reassuring. The warmth came from a gleaming red Aga stove with a kettle singing softly to itself on the hotplate and something else in a large pot giving off a delicious aroma, a blend of vegetables and herbs, reminding me that I had bypassed lunch.

A stout golden Labrador was stretched out on the mat warming her ample belly and snoring softly. In the high-backed wooden rocker just to the side of the stove a lion-sized ginger cat was deep in meditation. As we entered, the dog lifted her head, thumped her tail on the mat, then lumbered to her feet and padded across the room to offer polite greetings and examine me. The cat went on meditating.

'Sadie knows you are family,' both old people said in unison as the dog, her initial examination complete, wagged her tail vigorously and gave my outstretched hand a warm lick. A memory flash of my mother saying that she had never known the Ingrams disagree with each other and her talk of the Labradors of her childhood — no doubt ancestors of the friendly Sadie — gave me a feeling of déjà vu, almost as if I had been here before. I felt quite at home. I stroked the silky head of the dog and turned to Harry Ingram, who was explaining something.

'Dogs can always recognize members of a

family, even if they have never seen them before.'

Hilda Ingram gestured to one of the rush-seated ladder-backed chairs at the table (my years with Mum when she had her shop had given me a good knowledge of antiques). 'Sit down,' she urged.

I sat, resting my hands on the old kitchen table, its solidity covered with a bright gingham cloth, and let my eyes roam around the room feeling again that sense of coming home — of being where I belonged. In that moment I felt very close to my mother, almost as if her childhood memories of this room were my own. Hilda, as she put the large brown teapot on its stand on the table and wrapped it in a bright woolly cosy, brought me back to myself and the present.

'My, but it is good to see you sitting there!' She pulled the tray of scones towards her and splitting them deftly began buttering them with swift sure movements. 'Many's the time your mother sat right there and confided in me, told me her troubles as well as the good things, she did.' She sighed. 'I knew about your Dad right from the beginning, long before anyone else.'

While she was talking her husband had placed a tray on the table laid with a neat lace cloth, a cup and saucer, bowl of sugar and a dainty little teapot into which he was now pouring hot water. Hilda put some of the scones on a small plate and added it to the tray. 'There you are.' She nodded and with a small half-smile he picked up the tray and left the room.

I must have looked questioningly for she explained, 'That's for Miss Sybil.'

'Oh!' I said. Even as I wondered who Miss Sybil was and Hilda began to explain, I remembered Mum talking about an aunt, her father's sister, who lived at the Hall.

'Your Great-Aunt Sybil, I suppose she is. She's — well — you'll see for yourself if you stay here, I suppose.'

I supposed too, though it didn't seem clear yet whether I would have the chance to stay. I wondered where the rest of the family were as I bit into one of Hilda's delicious scones dripping with fresh butter. Fortunately I have a remarkable facility at times to enjoy the present moment.

Two cups of tea and a plate of scones later Hilda picked up the conversation more or less where we had dropped it. By this time Harry was back (my Australian upbringing made me think of him as this in my mind though I was careful to call him Mr Ingram when I spoke directly to him) and we were as cosy a little party as you could wish to find.

'As I was saying,' Hilda continued, 'your great-aunt lives here. She's a little — I suppose you could say . . . ' She tailed off.

'Eccentric, my dear,' Harry supplied. 'I think that is the word you are looking for.' He turned to me with a smile. 'But you needn't be bothered — *she* won't mind you.' Though this was comforting I found the accent on the word 'she' a tad disquieting.

A silence fell, and I, for one, was very much aware of my baggage lying out in the hall and the fact that if I couldn't stay here I would have to ask them to ring and order me a taxi to take me to a hotel. The two Ingrams looked at each other and I could see some sort of message flashing between them. Harry cleared his throat and Hilda put her hand across the table and laid it briefly on my arm.

'Harry will take your bags upstairs,' she told me. 'Put them in Miss Angie's room,' she instructed. 'We won't worry about anything till the rest of the family get back on Sunday, the day after tomorrow. Now I'll take you to see Miss Sybil.'

I followed Hilda back up the passage and into the main hall, feeling again that strange sense of being in a dream as I set foot on the bottom step of the magnificent flight of stairs that curved gently up to the landing which stood like a sort of gallery looking down on the hallway. Hilda paused here, I guess to get her breath back. I paused too and looked down onto the hall floor; from this vantage point the colour and pattern of the tiles was even more impressive. My mother's old nanny turned to me with an encouraging smile and what seemed almost like a squaring of her shoulders as if we were both facing some danger together. I found myself taking a deep breath as I followed her to one of the doors opening off the landing and stood behind her while she straightened her apron and knocked firmly on the polished wood of the heavy panelled door.

'Hello, Ozzie!' a raucous voice screeched as we stepped into the room. Naturally I thought it was directed at me and at first I thought it had come from the figure in the old-fashioned four-poster bed. It was an astonishing vision that gave a whole new meaning to the expression 'blue rinse generation'. The greeting was repeated and I saw that it was not the old lady in the bed but one of my compatriots, a Sulphur Crested Cockatoo, chained to a perch standing in the wide bay window. Apart from the fact that the bird, who I later learned was called 'Ozzie' because he was an Australian parrot, had a yellow topknot and the old lady's hair was rinsed to a wonderful shade of blue, the two bore a striking resemblance to each other; he with his sharp hooked beak and she with her hooked nose and strong chin giving her a nutcracker appearance. Added to that the keen dark eyes from which flashed a sharp intelligence in both cases that I felt I could be forgiven for thinking it was my great-aunt who had spoken.

Her eyes raked over me from head to toe and back again before she beckoned me to come closer. Her hand was wrinkled and the bony fingers tipped with long nails bore a marked similarity to the bird's feet as he moved his weight from one to the other on his perch flexing his long claws each time.

'So, you are Angela's daughter?' To my surprise and relief her voice was not at all like that of the parrot but was rich, unusually deep, and her accent was that of a cultured upper-class English woman what I privately thought of as 'a voice like the Queen's'. I stepped closer, remembering that my mother had always spoken of this aunt with a mixture of amusement and affection not untinged with respect. I smiled and, to our mutual astonishment, bent down and lightly kissed her cheek.

I stepped back quickly, somewhat overcome by my own temerity, but there was a definite twinkle in those keen eyes and the hint of a smile on her lips as she remarked, 'Demonstrative too — like your mother.' After a moment's scrutiny she turned to Hilda, still standing near the door. 'I think her mother's room, not the guest room, don't you?'

'I think so too.' A swift glance of conspiratorial agreement flashed between the two old ladies then Hilda picked up the tea tray and left me alone with my great-aunt.

'Now,' the old lady prompted as she settled back against her pillows to listen. 'Tell me everything — about yourself — why you are here, but most of all about your mother. Is she happy?'

I realized with a shock that she did not know my mother was dead. I could sense, rather than see, the frailness and vulnerability behind the 'tough old bird' exterior but there was no way I could tell her gently. Instinctively I moved closer and reached my hand out towards hers as I said, 'My mother is dead, Aunt Sybil.'

The hand on the quilt twitched as if it had a life of its own; I reached out further and let my fingers rest for a second on the parchment-dry skin. My throat ached and I could feel the tears pricking as I raised my eyes to hers and saw that they too were bright with unshed tears.

'I'm here because she asked me to come. I — I have a letter,' I told her, and turning away I fumbled in my bag and produced the sealed letter that my mother had left me when she died with instructions to give it to her family when — not if — I went to England.

She took the letter from my outstretched hand with fingers that trembled as they reached for it eagerly, almost hungrily. Raising my eyes to her face I saw her tighten her lips to control the tremor, and I could see that the tears were on the verge of falling. I turned away feeling like a voyeur. I would have left her then to read in peace but she held out a hand to stop me.

'No — don't go. I shall read this later when — when I haven't got you to talk to.' She pointed to a chair by the bed and managed a smile. 'Sit down and bring me up to date.' It was by way of a royal command. Obediently, I sat down wondering where to begin. 'Start at the end and work backwards,' she suggested seeing my hesitation. 'First, how did your mother die?'

'She had cancer. She went quite quickly at the end. I . . . ' My throat tightened and my voice broke as I remembered those last few weeks. 'She kept her business on till the last few months. I — I had no idea how sick she was when she first told me she was selling. I wish she had told me sooner. I — I would . . . ' I tailed off miserably. What would I have done? I don't really know how could things have been different. I looked up from the hanky I was twisting between my fingers and met those keen eyes that reminded me suddenly of my mother.

'Don't reproach yourself, my dear, I am sure there is no need, your mother was always independent, as I have every reason to know. I expect you were a great solace to her.' She disappeared briefly into herself then, with a sigh and a rather forced smile, continued, 'Tell me about her, what did she do and was she successful? And happy?'

'She had an antique shop, and yes, she was very successful, and I think happy.' I had never wondered before, just assumed it, accepted it. 'It was only in the months before she died that business began to fall away.' It was my turn now to retreat into my memories and, like her, I sighed as I added, 'Of course, I know now it was because she was sick. She had a wonderful eye for things and an amazing knowledge, I often wondered where it came from.'

'Look around this house and you will see where she got her first lessons. Your mother was surrounded by old and beautiful things from babyhood.'

'I suppose so,' I murmured.

'What about you, Maggie? Were you interested in the shop? Do you wish she had kept it on for you to run?'

I shook my head. 'Not really; I was interested, but not to the extent of actually wanting to run the business. Of course, I helped Mum out at weekends and holidays but it wasn't what I wanted to do full time.'

'And what did you want to do, or should I say do you want to do?' Aunt Sybil led me on gently.

'Photography. Ever since I got my first decent camera when I was eleven years old that is all I have ever wanted to do. From the time I was twelve I took all Mum's photos for her, for catalogues and advertisements and things,' I told her proudly, adding, 'I see photography as an art form — but of course you have to be really good to make a living that way.' I smiled apologetically. 'I realize I shall have to do some sort of commercial work to support myself.'

'What are you now, nineteen, twenty?' She hazarded an accurate guess.

'I was twenty a week ago.'

She nodded as if confirming this. 'What did you do when you left school?'

'I did a course in photography at my local TAFE College,' I told her. 'Then, well, the last six months or so I helped Mum sell up the business and, well, I sort of looked after her.' We were back again on those miserable last few months and I could feel the familiar tightening in my throat.

We sat together in silence, both lost in our own unhappy thoughts. Aunt Sybil was the first to break the silence. 'What made you come to England — what made you come here?' she asked.

Jerked out of my memories to the present by the sharpness in her voice I met her keen gaze unflinchingly. 'My mother asked me to. I can assure you that left to myself I would not have considered coming here.'

To my surprise the old lady gave a loud chortle that was, disconcertingly, immediately echoed by the parrot on his perch. I had forgotten his presence and this echo of her amusement made me turn in his direction.

'Don't mind Ozzie. I keep him because he always agrees with me.' I felt those keen eyes boring into me. 'Something I can see you are not likely to do!' I met her eyes, wondering if that meant she would not keep me and debating the wisdom of an apology, but before I could speak she continued, 'Don't worry; I like that. To tell you the truth Ozzie can be a bit dull as a conversationalist.' The slightly mocking smile faded as she reached out a tentative hand towards me. 'I like you, my dear. You have spirit — like your mother. I hope you will stay, for a while at least?'

I merely smiled in return, some innate cautiousness, even then, made me wary of committing myself.

'Go and settle in, unpack and make yourself at home. You have the place more or less to yourself for more than twenty-four hours, then . . . ' She tailed off and with another gesture of her hand dismissed me. As I turned from the door she was holding my mother's letter in her hand. I saw her sigh as she ran her nail under the seal. She told me later it merely introduced me as her daughter and hoped I would be welcome. Quietly, I slipped from the room.

3

Evening was settling round the house like a cloak as I made my way out to the landing. I searched for an electric light switch and flicked on the lights, they must have been of a very low wattage for they did little to dispel the grey shadows. However I did as my aunt had suggested and looked around. She was right, the place was full of antiques. I shivered slightly, not so much from the cold, but more as if I had been touched by a cold hand. The furniture may well have been valuable but it was also sombre. I made my way slowly down the magnificent staircase imagining myself sweeping down in the long full skirts of a bygone era, rather than serviceable jeans and my warmest sweater.

In the entrance hall I walked round and looked at the paintings and photographs that hung on the wood panelled walls. The photographs were nearly all black and white of people in old-fashioned dress, mostly stern and unsmiling. The paintings were of similar vintage and were, with one exception, hunting scenes. The one exception, an oil of a mare and foal, I thought I recognized as a

Stubbs, and close scrutiny proved me right. In pride of place in the centre was mounted a fox's head and on either side of it a bushy fox's tail. I shuddered, wondering how anyone could think that the preserved parts of a once beautiful and living animal ranked as ornament. There was more; in one corner of the hall stood a receptacle for sticks etc. Closer examination revealed that it had once been an elephant's foot! It was well filled with shooting sticks, riding crops, the odd walking stick and one large black umbrella.

I turned my attention to the photos, and was standing in front of one of the few colour ones, of a large, heavily built man dressed in white breeches, black boots, red coat and black velvet peaked cap, astride a horse which, even in the photo, appeared very large. The man had a large white moustache, and there was a confident arrogance about the way he sat on his horse. I thought he seemed the epitome of an English country gentleman with an army background. Though I must confess that up till now my acquaintance with such people was only between the covers of the novels I had read.

The feeling of familiarity that excited me and at the same time filled me with foreboding did not, however, stem from a previous meeting in a book. I was uncomfortably sure I knew who he was even before Mr Ingram's voice startled me by confirming: 'That was taken of your grandfather when he was Master of the Hunt.'

I spun round in the direction of the voice. The old man was standing in the archway of the passage that led down to the kitchen regions. His gaze, I noted, went straight past me to the man in the photo.

'A week after that photo was taken he had the fall.' He spoke in such sombre tones that I thought the worst.

'Was — was it serious?' I trailed off, for some reason having just been told this formidable looking gentleman on his splendid horse was my grandfather, I found it hard to ask 'is he dead?'

Mr Ingram shook his head as if I had spoken the words aloud. 'He's in a wheelchair. Never walked since.'

'Oh.' I turned back to the painting, feeling somewhat guilty to discover I felt more concern for the horse than my grandfather. And as if I had actually asked the question aloud, the old man supplied the answer.

'Huntsman broke a leg and was shot.'

'Oh.' Once again, all I could find to say was this ridiculously inadequate monosyllable. I gave an involuntary little shiver and turned away from the photo that had induced in me feelings both of depression and something else that I couldn't quite put my finger on. Fear seemed altogether too strong a word, and yet . . . I gave a small shudder and moved towards the bright rectangle of light at the head of the passageway, the kitchen with its warmth and homeliness felt like a good place to be. But as I moved towards it Mr Ingram's voice changed my direction.

'I've put your bags in Miss Angela's old room, Miss Maggie.' He walked across the hall towards the stairs as he spoke. 'If you will come with me I'll show you which room it is.'

There seemed little choice but to follow so I once more climbed the staircase towards the upper landing which was only a tad less gloomy than the hall. We passed my great-aunt's room and at the far end of the landing Mr Ingram flung open another heavy oak door. I followed him into the room. I don't think anything had been changed in all the years since my mother walked out of it for the last time. I sensed the very essence of her, almost as if she were still there. It did not alarm me, on the contrary I found it comforting, it helped me to feel at home in the vast cold space. Hilda must have been in, for someone had pulled the chintz curtains closed and two thick white towels hung over the wooden towel rack and a single bar electric heater had been switched on. It looked cheerful but made little impression on the arctic temperature in the room.

'The bathroom is along the corridor.' Mr Ingram's voice reminded me that he was still there. 'Dinner will be ready in about an hour, Hilda said to tell you.'

I nodded and mumbled a brief 'thanks', suddenly overcome with emotion that I was actually here, in the room that my mother had called her own until she ran away from everything she knew to marry my father. For the first time I had some inkling of the enormity of what she had done. Fighting back a sudden rush of tears I took my toilet things from my overnight bag and headed for the bathroom.

Here I felt I had stepped into a time warp, and yet there was also that sense of not quite recalled familiarity. Almost as if I actually remembered the deep bath on claw feet, and the toilet, up a couple of wooden steps on a little dais, a throne indeed. The cistern rumbled and gurgled ominously. There was no heating; this was not a place to linger.

Back in the bedroom I quickly took a few clothes out of my case. As I pushed the old-fashioned eiderdown back to put my pyjamas under the pillow I discovered a stone hot water bottle between the sheets explaining the odd bump I had already noticed. I prudently switched off the heater and hurried downstairs to the warm kitchen. I found it redolent with the scent of good cooking, guaranteed to set my young and healthy digestive juices working, and by the time I joined the old couple at the table I was ready to do justice to the meal.

In spite of their welcome and kindness I could not help but feel both curious and apprehensive about the rest of the family and how they would react to my presence. My thoughts flew to Tim Fenton and I felt a glow as I remembered how he had taken me under his wing. I forgot for the moment that I had found his conviction that I needed his help annoying and only remembered his kindness.

'I wonder — do you think I could use the phone this evening?' I asked as we ate, directing my question to Mr Ingram who seemed to me to have an unassailable air of authority. But, as so often happens it was Hilda who answered my question while he was gathering his words to reply.

'Why — of course! You don't need to ask permission, you are a member of the family, you know.'

'Thanks.' I nodded, wondering again about this family, hitherto unknown to me, that I had walked into.

'Mother hardly ever talked about her

family,' I said now, adding with a smile that embraced both my companions, 'In fact she talked more about you two. Perhaps you could put me in the picture — tell me something about them — who lives here, other than Aunt Sybil?'

They glanced at each other before Hilda began, 'Well, there's your grandfather, of course.'

'You mean?' I looked across at Mr Ingram.

He nodded. 'Yes, the one whose photo you were looking at.'

'He's — '

'Yes, he's in a wheelchair. It's unusual for him not to be home — seldom goes anywhere, but for some reason he decided to go to this wedding.' The old man shook his head as if still wondering what had made my grandfather behave out of character.

'Well, it was his grandson's wedding,' Hilda reminded him.

'Yes, well. Then there is your Aunt Natalie — your mother's sister and . . . '

Here I interrupted her. 'Sister? Did you say — my mother's sister? I didn't know she had one.' It was true — I could not ever remember my mother referring to a sister. This seemed astonishing, even allowing for the fact that my mother had left home under a cloud.

'They didn't get on.' Hilda's lips tightened and her voice was expressionless. 'But of course they were not really sisters, your Aunt Natalie was your mother's step-sister. Her mother was your grandfather's second wife. Natalie and Gerald were a little bit older than your mother when your grandfather married their mother.'

'So, my mother had a step-brother too?' I asked, amazed that this was the first time I had heard of any of these people. 'What about my step-grandmother?' I supposed that was the correct relationship.

'Dead.' Mr Ingram shot the single word into the conversation. I looked from one to the other; from their blank and stony expressions I didn't think they were sorry about it.

'Are — are there any more?' I asked somewhat hesitantly.

'Oh, yes. Your Aunt Natalie has a husband and two sons and your Uncle Gerald has twin daughters just going into their teens. It was Simon, one of your Aunt Natalie's sons, who got married this weekend.'

'Oh,' I said somewhat blankly. I was feeling slightly stupefied to discover that I, who so short a time ago had been virtually alone in the world, now had so many relatives.

Hilda and Mr Ingram devoted the rest of

the meal to 'putting me in the picture' about my family. At least that is what they thought they were doing. In reality I was getting more confused by the minute. I wished I had a biro in my hand and a pad in front of me instead of a fork and a plate! As they chattered on I began to feel not only confused but also even more apprehensive about meeting up with this family of mine, and almost wished I had never followed my mother's dying wish and come to England to seek them out. If I could have seen into the future I think I might well have left the house there and then, certainly first thing the next morning, and forgotten all about them.

I insisted on helping Hilda dry the dishes and tidy up after our meal before tentatively mentioning the phone again.

'Good gracious me, girl, you don't have to ask if you can use the phone!' she exclaimed as she dried her hands.

'But — ' I began hesitantly.

'Of course, you don't know where it is. Show her, Harry.'

I followed the old man up the long passage from the kitchen into the main entrance hall. He switched on the light over a corner alcove to reveal a small cupboard that he opened with a flourish, rather like a magician extracting a rabbit from a hat, and there, on a

41

shelf, stood the telephone.

'Thanks! I must say that's pretty cute, I've never seen a phone kept in a cupboard before.'

He didn't acknowledge my attempt at light conversation beyond the faintest nod as he warned me there were three extensions: 'One in the master's study and another in Miss Sybil's room.'

'And?' I prompted gently; he seemed to have stopped at this point without telling me where the third extension was located. The old man turned away from the cupboard and turned back towards the kitchen and I thought maybe he had not heard. I was about to repeat my question when he turned slowly on his heel.

'The third extension is in Mrs Sinclair's room,' he told me in a deadpan voice.

'Oh.' Yet again I resorted to the single syllable, wondering why his words, delivered as they were in a voice totally devoid of emotion, should send a shiver down my spine. Or maybe it was just the coldness of the hall.

'Thank you,' I repeated to his retreating back and turned to pick up the receiver.

I had Tim's card in my pocket; the light was not good but I deciphered the number and carefully dialled, only to realize that I had got an answering machine. A woman's voice was informing me courteously that I could leave a message or my number after the beep. I was about to do just that when Tim's voice came on the line.

'Is that you, Tim? For real? I mean not an answering service . . . ' I babbled rather foolishly. 'It's Maggie here — Maggie Townsend. Remember . . . ' My voice trailed off as I realized that though it may seem an age ago it was actually only this morning that we had parted company. He would wonder what had prompted me to ring him so soon.

'Hi! Great to hear you — I was just walking in the door when I heard the answering service start so I cut in. How are you? Did you get to your relations OK?'

I was reassured by the friendly note in his voice. 'Yes, I found my way here in one piece and I'm as well as I was when I left you this morning,' I added with a rather shaky laugh. Impossible to believe it was less than twenty-four hours since I had parted from Tim. I hoped my calling him wouldn't convince him I was some sort of helpless clinging female that having once rescued he would never get rid of again.

'It's good to hear you,' he repeated. 'I've been thinking about you — wondering if you made it out to the ancestral castle, or whatever.'

'Not exactly a castle, but, yes — I'm here. I just wanted to thank you for being so helpful.' *And to hear your voice*, I might have added.

'Think nothing of it.' He brushed my thanks aside. 'Look, I'm going to be up in the Midlands later in the week. I'll call you and we'll get together.'

'I'd like that,' I told him, hoping my voice didn't give away just how much I would like it.

'I have to go now,' he told me. 'You only just caught me. I ran back in to get something I'd left behind and there you were!'

I stood for a moment just holding the receiver in my hand listening to the impersonal brrrr after he rang off. I wondered if he would call, or if that was just a nice brush-off and I would never hear from him again. I replaced the receiver slowly, as jet lag hit me like a sledgehammer. Suddenly I was just so tired that I could hardly bring myself to walk down that long passage to the kitchen and bid the Ingrams goodnight.

'I'm going to turn in,' I told them, sticking my head round the door. 'I'm just about beat.'

Hilda looked up, dropping her hands full of knitting in her lap. 'Yes,' her voice was kind, 'I can see that. I shan't call you in the morning so you can sleep on. No one is expected back till the day after tomorrow.'

I smiled my thanks and wishing them both goodnight, made my way upstairs to my own room. I reflected gratefully as I settled between the warm sheets, that the old-fashioned stone hottie had done a good job. I pushed it down the bed to warm my feet and wondered if this same bottle had comforted my mother on cold nights. My last conscious thought was gratitude that I had a few more hours grace before meeting up with my new family.

I yawned, stretched and looked at my watch. Eleven-thirty? Surely not, if so I must have slept for about fifteen hours. When I jumped out of bed to open the curtains the cold in the room hit me with a physical shock as if I had dived into cool water. I gasped as I pulled back the heavy material. The pale February sun was glinting on the fern-like patterns of frost on the window panes and the garden below was sparkling with a thick covering of snow and hoar frost. It was more than an unusual sight for me, it was breathtakingly beautiful.

I dressed quickly in the warmest clothes I could find and hurried downstairs towards the kitchen. Here I was greeted by warmth, the rich smell of cooking and the even more welcome one of coffee from a pot that was percolating in a desultory fashion on the Aga.

Hilda turned round from the sink where she was busy doing something with a mound of vegetables. Her smile was warm. She nodded in the direction of the coffee pot.

'There's a mug, sugar and milk on the table. Help yourself. If you would prefer tea . . . ' She nodded at the kettle simmering gently on the hob.

'Coffee is fine,' I assured her as I poured myself a large mug and inhaled the rich aroma with delight. 'I'll skip food,' I said, even though my inside felt quite hollow. It must, after all, have been nearly lunchtime.

'Better have some toast, at least.' Hilda advised me, pointing with her paring knife at the toaster with a loaf of bread sitting beside it. 'Lunch won't be till one o'clock as Mrs Sinclair phoned at breakfast time to say they would be back for lunch today after all.' With a small sigh she returned to the vegetables she was preparing.

Maybe she was right, I reflected, and dropped a couple of slices into the toaster. It looked as if I was going to come face to face with my family sooner than I had bargained for, so I had better keep my strength up. Watching Hilda doggedly peeling and slicing as I ate, it struck me that she didn't appear any more overjoyed than I was at the prospect of the family returning a few hours earlier than expected. She firmly refused my offers of help so when I had finished eating I donned parka, gloves and the strongest shoes I had and made my way out to explore the garden.

There was not much to see as everything was blanketed in snow though that in itself was a novelty for me. I walked briskly along an icy path and through an archway that in the summer probably dropped rose petals but now only dripped snowflakes down my neck. I headed back towards the house. However visually pleasing it was this extreme cold was hard to take, used as I was to my sun-baked homeland.

After stamping my feet hard on the doormat I made my way back up to my room. As I passed the door of my great-aunt's bedroom I paused, suddenly feeling alone in this large strange house. I felt I would like to talk to someone — anyone — even Ozzie would do!

As I hesitated with my hand raised I heard his raucous voice followed by my aunt's much pleasanter tones: 'Who is there? Is it you, Maggie?'

Astonished, I opened the door and went in. 'Hello,' I said, 'I was just outside the door wondering whether I would be disturbing you if I knocked. How did you know it was me?'

'Ozzie told me. When he shrieks in that particular way I know someone is outside the door; I guessed it would be you as I hadn't seen you yet today.'

'I — I didn't like to disturb you,' I muttered, guilty for doing just that. It hadn't occurred to me that she might actually like to see me.

'Well, now you are here, come along and talk to me, tell me what you think of the house before the mob gets home.'

I moved closer to the bed. 'It's very big,' I began tentatively, 'well, compared with Australian houses anyway, and — and . . . '

'Very cold. Is what you also would like to say?'

I smiled. 'Well — yes. It's also full of some very lovely old things. I certainly know where my mother got her grounding in antiques.' I could have added that I also found the house in some strange way oppressive but tact bid me hold my tongue.

My answer seemed to satisfy her for she smiled at me with real warmth and for an instant I was reminded of my mother. 'Come and have afternoon tea with me,' she invited, 'and you can tell me what you think of all your relations.' She chortled to herself and looked at me with rather malicious amusement. 'I wonder what they are going to make of you.' Then she touched my hand and smiled and I knew her malice was not directed at me. 'You are going to be a bit of a surprise to them I think; in fact, I could say you are going to cause quite a few ripples. I would say 'the cat among the pigeons' except that I am half afraid it may be the other way round, a pigeon among the cats.'

I had barely closed the door behind me and was about to go along to my own room when I heard the sound of car doors slamming and voices growing louder as the front door was flung wide. I peered over the banisters to the hall below.

There seemed a great many people coming in through the door, among them my grandfather in his wheelchair. Both Ingrams and Sadie the labrador were there to greet the family. Up here on the landing I felt as if I had a grandstand seat in a theatre. Maybe it was this illusion that made me oblivious of the fact that I was as visible to the people down below as they were to me. At that moment one of the younger members of the party, a teenage girl, looked up and saw me. I saw her nudge the girl at her side, who was, I realized, her double. Obviously these were the twins, and perfectly in unison they both called out: 'Who are you?' causing the others in the group to follow their gaze.

I stepped back from the railing wishing that I had not allowed my curiosity to get the better of me. Well, this was the decisive moment. I squared my chin and descended the staircase with as much aplomb and dignity as I could muster with the eyes of the entire family on me. I noticed Hilda saying something to the tall, elegant woman who stood by my grandfather's wheelchair. It was the longest flight of stairs I had ever walked down.

'I am Maggie Townsend,' I said as I reached the hall, directing my words to the patriarchal figure in the wheelchair. 'My mother . . . '

'I know perfectly well who your mother is, what I would like to know is what you are doing here and who invited you?'

He didn't wait for an answer but turned his back on me and, gripping the wheels of his chair with strong hands, propelled himself towards the swing door to the right of the hall. With a swwwsh it swung shut behind him and I was left, silent and tongue-tied in the midst of my newfound relatives, rejected and humiliated by the one who mattered most — my grandfather.

4

My silence seemed both contagious and tangible, like some sort of a blanket hanging round us all. I was the first to speak. 'Hi!' I said, and was appalled to hear the squeak in my voice, but at least I had broken the silence.

'Hello!' 'When did you get here?' Have you come all the way from Australia?' They all seemed to be speaking at once now and I glanced from face to face to see who was saying what. To add to my confusion it seemed that the only two people speaking were the twins. I looked from one to the other, they were so identical I wondered how they even knew each other! From them I turned my attention to the adults who seemed to be standing in a circle looking at me. Two middle-aged women and two men, one the same vintage as the women and the other much younger. The latter was looking me over appraisingly. To my annoyance I felt myself flush but managed to meet, and hold, his gaze.

'We-ell!' he drawled. 'And where did you spring from?'

I was spared the necessity of answering by what I judged to be the elder of the two women stepping forward with outstretched hand.

'So you are Maggie?' I nodded. 'I'm Natalie Talbot, your mother's step-sister, so I suppose I am your step-aunt.'

I murmured, 'I supposed so too.'

She turned round to the other members of the family. 'Let me introduce you. This is my son, Nigel Talbot, my other son, Simon, is on his honeymoon. My brother Gerald de Witt, his wife Sophie and their daughters, Josephine and Jacqueline.'

I nodded, smiling to each in turn but the only one who really smiled back, with her eyes as well as her lips, was Sophie. I felt myself warm to her. The welcome from the others seemed about as frosty as the air outside.

'Welcome to the ancestral home!' Natalie said. Did I imagine the irony in her voice? 'I suggest we all have a drink before lunch and get to know one another!' With that she led the way towards the dining-room.

Here her husband took charge, he picked up the sherry decanter from the sideboard, and with an all embracing though rather vague, smile asked, 'Sherry everyone?' Without waiting for an answer he began pouring. I have never really liked sherry but felt it would be churlish to refuse, when everyone had a glass he raised his in my direction. 'To our new relative!'

'To our new found cousin!' his son, Nigel, corrected as he raised his glass in my direction and gave me a mock bow.

I took a gulp — rather than a sip — and nearly choked. My discomfiture was not helped by the knowledge that everyone seemed to be looking at me, especially my step-cousin Nigel who watched with sardonic amusement. I vowed that in future I would have the courage to say, 'No thank you!'

Into the silence Sophie, my other step-aunt by marriage, said that she would go and see what Father was doing and if he wanted any lunch and tell Hilda she could serve. She was, I realized the only one of my new relatives who had not actually spoken to me. Even as the thought came into my mind I looked up and met her gaze upon me as she put down her sherry glass and turned to leave the room. The flash of fear in the light grey eyes that only moments before had smiled at me caused me to catch my breath in much the same way that the dry sherry had a few seconds earlier. She held my gaze for the briefest of moments then abruptly left the room.

I do not know what I had expected from these people, the nearest I had in the world to a family, but it had certainly not been the open hostility I had been shown by my grandfather and the odd reaction of the woman who appeared to be a sort of step-aunt.

In spite of the fact that I found the very dry sherry most unpalatable, I drained my glass before taking the seat at the long polished table indicated to me by Natalie. I found myself with Nigel on my left and Gerald, at the head of the table, on my right. Directly opposite me were the twins. I wondered which of the two women would take the place at the other end of the table. Neither in fact did; Natalie sat on Nigel's left and when Sophie returned she took the seat next to Josephine, or Jacqueline.

The meal itself was an excellent roast with vegetables which, being young and hungry I could not help but enjoy though I found the atmosphere round the table curious, to say the least. The twins addressed most of their conversation to each other occasionally shooting a question across the table at me — questions, I felt which either showed their lamentable ignorance of Australia or were intended to belittle me. I rather suspected the latter. When one of them asked me if we had computers in

Australia, Gerald muttered a vague protest but their mother Sophie merely allowed a slight smile to play about her lips. When she had taken her seat at the table Natalie had leaned across with some query, I presumed about my grandfather, for Sophie replied that he was having his lunch in his room.

By the time the meal was over I was wondering how I could make my escape graciously from this household. It seemed so obvious that I had no place here; and yet they were all the family I had. Looking round the table at them I felt a leaden ache of disappointment. Growing up an only child I had built up these unknown relations on the other side of the world into some sort of dream family. The reality was hard to accept. I did my best to join in the conversation but as most of it was about events and people I knew nothing of it was not easy. I had drifted off into my own thoughts when I realized that I was being asked a question by one of the twins.

'Er, sorry,' I mumbled. 'I didn't quite catch what you said.'

'Hunting — we were talking about. Do you hunt?'

I must have looked pretty blank because she said with what I could only describe as 'synthetic' patience, 'I suppose you do have fox-hunting in Australia?'

'Er, no — I mean, yes.' I could have bitten my tongue out. That was the second time I had started a sentence with 'Er' and my contradictory answer could hardly be called intelligent. I sat there tongue-tied, frantically racking my brain for what, if anything, I knew about fox-hunting in Australia.

'Of course they do!' It was Nigel coming to my rescue. 'There is the Melbourne Hunt Club and the Sydney Hunt Club. They hunt in Tasmania too — but not foxes because there aren't any there, so they have drag hunts. Foxes were actually imported to Australia by the early gentry who missed their fox-hunting here. Just like they are going to here now it is banned by the government.'

By now I was gaping at him, partly in gratitude and amazement and partly in annoyance at myself. I had known all that about Australia, why on earth couldn't I have trotted it out instead of sitting dumbstruck while he did? I managed to smile however and nodded in agreement. 'Yes, that is correct about Australia; but is it true that it has been banned here?'

'It's just too stupid,' one of the twins said with a sulky pout.

'Do you hunt?' The other twin now asked me again.

I shook my head. 'I don't live near any hunt club.' Well, that was true anyway. No need to add that if I had lived in the very centre of hunting country it was still most unlikely that I would have had the money (or the inclination) to take part in what I privately considered a barbaric and outmoded sport designed for the snobbish rich. I wished I had the courage to quote Oscar Wilde's famous comment about fox-hunting being the 'unspeakable' in pursuit of the 'uneatable'.

'I suppose you can ride?' There was a barely veiled insolence on the face of the twin asking the question that made my hackles rise. Once again Nigel answered for me while I was still opening my mouth.

'Of course she can. All Australians ride!'

Fortunately it was partly true, I could ride; in fact it had been one of my childhood passions and I had spent every Saturday morning at the local riding school and later enjoyed some wonderful trail-riding holidays.

'What have you done with your horse?' one of the twins now asked.

I looked at her blankly. Surely she didn't think I had ridden a horse from Australia! 'Horse?' I said stupidly.

'Yes — what did you do with it when you came to England. Is someone else looking after it or did you sell it?'

'I don't have one, so no problem.' I somehow made it sound as if not having a horse was only a temporary state of affairs and not the absolute norm for me. Riding lessons and holidays were one thing; actually owning a horse was something Mum's income had never run to.

My answer must have been satisfactory for as we finally rose from the table and the adults drifted away I was invited by the twins, this time in unison, to come out to the stables and see the horses. I mumbled my acquiescence and appreciation, then turned in surprise as I heard Nigel's voice just behind me: I had thought he had left the room with the others.

'Put a coat on and change your shoes,' he was advising me. I glanced out the window at the wintry scene then down at my feet clad in light indoor pumps and nodded.

'I'll just run up and change.'

'See you in the hall!' Did he intend to come too?

As I ran quickly back along the landing after grabbing my parka and pushing my feet into a more solid pair of shoes, I noticed that my Aunt Sibyl's door was open. I hesitated, wondering whether I should stick my head in and say a quick hello when she called out. 'Is that you, Maggie? Come in!'

I pushed open the door to be greeted by a raucous shout from Ozzie.

'Oh! You're going out?' The old lady sounded disappointed.

'Only out to the stables — the twins have asked me to see the horses,' I told her.

'The horses!' she repeated after me and there was no mistaking the yearning in her voice. 'Are you a good horsewoman — like your mother?'

I gaped. 'Like my mother?' I repeated stupidly. My mother had never even told me she could ride.

'Oh yes — she was one of the best horse-women in the family. After me of course!'

I looked at her, uncertain whether or not she was joking, it seemed even more impossible to imagine this exotic old lady on a horse than to accept that my mother had also been a good horsewoman. But I saw that she was quite serious and that her expression was one of nostalgia as she remembered past glories. As I looked at her she seemed to give herself a sort of mental shake and came abruptly back to the present.

'Well, I won't keep you. Go along and meet the horses, and come back later and tell me all about them.' Thus dismissed I smiled my farewell and hurried to my cousins in the hall.

I found the three of them waiting for me. They all looked far better prepared for the rigours of the great outdoors in the middle of an English winter than I was. I saw a quick glance pass between the twins and guessed it was an unspoken comment on my appearance. I wondered how long it would take for me to learn which was Jacqueline and which Josephine — even if I wanted to, for their hostility was still obvious. I was glad of Nigel's presence and even though he also seemed to look me over I didn't feel he was critical. In fact, when I met his glance and he smiled I was able to smile back with genuine warmth.

We tramped out over the crisp frosty snow and round to the stable block at the back of the house. I sniffed appreciatively, the familiar horse smell bringing back golden days of my childhood. I remembered my weekends mucking out, grooming and escorting rides in exchange for extra time in the saddle, as some of the happiest days of my life, when Mum was fit and well and the future bright with promise.

The stable block was half a dozen spacious loose boxes and a tack room looking out on a cobbled yard. From each of the stables a horse watched our approach with interest. Even I, who was no expert on horse flesh, could appreciate that these were a cut above the riding school hacks that I had known. Seeing my genuine appreciation the twins' attitude towards me warmed slightly especially as I had unwittingly given particular praise to their own two horses.

Both were greys with soft flowing manes and fine muzzles, they were almost as alike as their owners. When I commented on this Nigel murmured, 'But of course! If they had different coloured horses we might be able to tell them apart!' He put his hand on my elbow and steered me towards the end box where a handsome chestnut with a white blaze looked out on us. He gave a soft whicker as we approached and, rummaging in his pocket, Nigel produced a lump of sugar. 'This is Sportsman,' he told me, almost as if he were formally introducing a person. He turned back and rubbed the horse's face with his forefinger and I felt my heart warm towards him as I watched.

'He's very handsome!' I said, 'and very like the horse in the photo in the hall — the one with . . . ' I paused, somehow finding it hard to refer to that stern and forbidding figure in the wheelchair as 'Grandfather'.

'He is his full brother,' Nigel told me, 'Huntsman and Sportsman, almost as alike as Jackie and Josie!' This was the second time in a few minutes that he had referred to the uncanny likeness between the twins. As he spoke he shot a malicious glance at them and I noticed they both coloured up slightly and one bit her bottom lip as if cutting off a sharp retort. This surprised me, as they seemed to have no reservations themselves about using the fact that they were difficult to distinguish to disconcert other people, so why should they mind Nigel's comments? I pushed such thoughts to the back of my mind as I walked from box to box admiring and talking to the inmates. I noticed that all except two, a little dark brown mare and a woolly pony of around twelve hands, were well rugged.

'Do you keep them in all winter?' I asked.

'But of course!'

'They are stabled for the season.'

As usual the twins answered in unison.

'We used to keep them fit for the hunting season,' Nigel explained. 'We don't seem able to lose the habit.'

'What about these two?' I asked looking over the half door at the brown mare and the pony.

'Oh, they aren't used much now. They are only in temporarily because of the snow.' Nigel's tone dismissed them as of no further interest. But there was something about the mare that attracted me. She had come tentatively to the door and was sniffing my hand with a soft velvet muzzle, her breath warm on my fingers.

'They are both pretty ancient now,' one of the twins explained. 'We all learned to ride on old Peggy and Colleen was Aunt Sybil's and she hasn't ridden for yonks!'

Reluctantly I turned away from the two in the box and continued my guided tour of the other stables and their occupants. While I duly admired, the twins quizzed me, none too subtly, on the extent of my riding ability and experience.

'I suppose you rode on Western saddles?' Jackie, or was it Josie, asked as she opened the door of the tack room.

'No,' I told her, 'mostly Poly or Stock saddles.'

'What on earth are those?' the other twin, Josie, or Jackie, wanted to know.

'They are peculiarly Australian, my dear cuz,' Nigel drawled in what I had to admit was a passable imitation of an Australian accent. Seeing the half smile playing about my lips he added, 'Specially designed to keep the rider in the saddle when chasing cows or sheep. Isn't that so, Maggie?'

'Well yes, I guess so,' I admitted, thinking how bare the highly polished English saddles ranged neatly on their racks seemed after the deep comfortable saddles with their knee pads and thigh rolls I had been used to. 'Maybe they would be equally good for chasing foxes!' I could not resist saying. 'Except of course you don't do that now, but they *are* good for keeping you in the saddle.'

Both twins laughed and to my surprise Nigel coloured, whether with embarrassment or annoyance I was not sure.

'Yes Nigel,' They said in that disconcerting way they had of speaking in unison. 'Maybe you should have one, save you falling in the mud in front of Lydia Hamilton!' It seemed I had unwittingly scored a point. As we walked back to the house Nigel was silent, almost sulky, but both girls chatted happily, even drawing me into the conversation now and then.

Passing Aunt Sybil's door on the way to my own room I paused. She had asked me to come back and report to her after I had seen the horses. Tentatively I knocked and her voice immediately called to me to come in. I was surprised to see the bed empty and the old lady sitting upright in a magnificent armchair, more like a throne, in the big window. She indicated a smaller chair placed opposite her own and I crossed the room and sat down.

'You are up!' I exclaimed, trying to sound

pleased rather than surprised.

'I am up!' she repeated. 'I am not quite as decrepit as they all think — and hope!'

'Oh, surely not! I mean — you're not decrepit at all — and I'm sure they don't think you are and certainly wouldn't hope . . . ' I floundered to a halt before her piercing eyes and sardonic smile.

'Of course they do! And I let them — it quite suits me at times,' she said with asperity. 'Now, sit down, tell me about the horses, particularly my old Colleen, how did she look? Are they looking after her in this dreadful weather? Is she rugged? Sit there.' She pointed again to the smaller chair which I now saw had a thick photograph album lying on the seat. 'Tell me about her,' she repeated. 'Then I'll show you some photos.'

'She looks well, and she is in a stable with the pony,' I told her 'But no — she isn't rugged.' I saw a shadow cross her face and added hastily, 'She is still a very lovely horse. How old is she?'

'You are thinking that if I rode her she must be pretty ancient! You are right, of course. She must be — let me see — somewhere well in her twenties now. But it isn't so long ago that I was riding her.' She pulled herself up in her chair and there was a glow in her cheeks and her eyes shone with the memory so that for a moment I forgot she was old. 'Pass me the album,' she commanded, 'and I will show you.'

She turned the pages quickly and soon found the one she wanted. She passed it over to me. 'We were both twenty years younger then and had just won the Ladies Hack class at the County Show.' I gazed at the photo of a truly regal figure seated side saddle on one of the loveliest horses I had ever seen. How sad, I thought, that people and horses both had to age.

'Turn back a few pages,' she ordered, 'and you will see a photo of a horse jumping. It's an excellent photo, just caught at the perfect moment when the horse was absolutely horizontal over the jump.'

I did as she told me and had no difficulty finding the photo, which was, as she said, truly excellent. I wondered who the rider was; even under the riding hat it was obvious she was fairly young, around the twins' age I guessed.

'Do you recognize the rider?' she asked me.

I shook my head, unless . . . 'Is it — ?'

'Your mother,' she interrupted me. 'She would have been in her teens then. I told you she was an accomplished horsewoman.'

I peered at the photo, trying to recognize the mother I had known in this girl pictured when she was my own age or younger. But interested as I was in the personal aspect of the photo my professional attention was also caught. This was a masterly picture, taken by an expert, everything about it was right, the light, the exposure, most of all the perfect timing to catch the horse in mid-flight. There was a name at the bottom of the picture. I peered at it: Townsend — my own name. I looked up, a question in my eyes as well as one forming on my lips.

'Yes,' my aunt told me. 'He took it — your father. In fact that is how your mother met him — through that picture.' Her eyes had taken on a glazed look and I knew that she was looking back into the past.

'I didn't know — I never knew . . . ' I floundered to a halt as I realized that she was listening to her own thoughts not my words. It was true, I had never known that my mother could even ride a horse, let alone ride like this, and though I had known my father was a photographer I had never realized that it had been anything but a hobby with him. At least it explained my own love of what I considered an art form and my mother's reluctance for me to take it up as a career. But why, I wondered, had I never been told these things till now? It did not cross my mind then to wonder why my great-aunt had chosen to inform me, only why my mother had not. Suddenly I was angry that I should be so ignorant of my own heritage and became determined to learn more, but even as I opened my mouth to speak there was a knock on the door and Aunt Sybil snapped the book shut with a curt 'Come in!' and Hilda entered with a tea tray.

5

'I have just taken the afternoon tea trolley into the lounge, Miss Maggie.' Hilda told me as she fussed about, moving a small table closer to my aunt and setting the tray down on it. Her words and the finality with which the old lady had snapped the photo album shut were a clear dismissal. I left, thinking that I would not bother with tea and started towards my own room. As I did so I heard the sound of the phone ringing somewhere below. My hand was on the knob of my bedroom door when I heard my name called, also from somewhere down in the well of the hall. Turning, I went to the banisters and leaned over. 'Yes?' I asked the upturned face of one of the twins.

'You are wanted on the phone,' she shouted up to me. 'Someone called Fenton.'

Tim! He was on the phone. I raced down the stairs as fast as I could, almost tumbling over my own feet and myself in my eagerness to get there. I was quite breathless and my heart was thumping, whether with exertion or simple pleasure I wasn't sure, by the time I snatched the receiver from the girl's outstretched hand and gasped a breathy 'Hello' into it. I turned slightly, aware that Jackie, or Josie, was still there watching — and listening. My glare must have been suitably intimidating, for with a light shrug, she turned and walked away.

'Tim? How good to hear you!' My delight sounded overdone, even to myself.

'Good to hear you, too!' He didn't seem to notice — or mind. 'Look, I'm going to be up in your part of the world tomorrow — got an assignment. Thought maybe we could meet? Lunch perhaps?'

'Oh, yes. I'd love that!' I tried hard not to sound too eager. 'What time — er — where?' In spite of myself the words came tumbling out, betraying my excitement. Only when I had said them did it cross my mind that I had no means of getting anywhere. But Tim said he would pick me up.

'Around eleven o'clock?' he suggested, adding, 'That's tomorrow, OK?'

'OK!' I assured him. 'I'll be ready!' I added as he said goodbye before hanging up.

I was still standing there, the receiver in my hand, listening to its brrrr with a curious sense of loss when Nigel's voice made me start. 'Boyfriend?' he asked.

'No — No,' I told him. 'Just a — a friend.'

Replacing the receiver I smiled my acknowledgement.

'Tea trolley is in the lounge, are you coming?' he asked.

I followed him, repressing the unkind thought that he had been in the hall more to listen in to my conversation than to call me for tea. Yet it did seem as if we walked into an unnaturally silent room and I felt all eyes were upon me waiting for an explanation of my phone call. I would like to have held my own counsel but common politeness dictated that I should at least tell them I would be going out for the day tomorrow.

'A friend is picking me up tomorrow to take me out for lunch, I hope that is all right?' I addressed myself to Sophie.

'But of course.' Her tone was smooth. 'How nice — is it someone you know from Australia?'

'Yes,' I lied. Adding with more truth, 'He is here working.' I had no intention of volunteering the information that I hadn't even known of the existence of Tim Fenton when I boarded the plane in Australia.

There was a pause while this piece of information was digested then the family resumed their conversation. I let it flow around me, so that in my own little private cocoon of silence I could savour the delicious

71

thought of meeting up with Tim again in less than twenty-four hours' time. As soon as I could I escaped to my room. Crossing the gloomy hall I cast a longing look in the direction of the door behind which, I knew, lay the passage that ended in the warmth and brightness of the kitchen. I looked round almost guiltily then on an impulse I turned to my left instead of heading up the staircase.

I found both the Ingrams sitting at the big kitchen table, a large brown teapot between them.

'Miss Maggie!' Hilda jumped to her feet looking both surprised and shocked. I gestured to her to sit down.

'Please!' I begged. 'Just Maggie!' I looked round me appreciatively. 'Oh,' I said with a sigh. 'It's much nicer here!' Indeed it was, here there was warmth of quite another kind than the actual physical warmth in the other room. I saw Hilda glance at her husband. I didn't mind because there was none of the antagonism I felt when I saw members of my family glance at one another in my presence.

'I don't think they are very pleased to see me,' I admitted ruefully. After all, even though they were total strangers they were my family. Neither of the Ingrams attempted to contradict me; they just looked at me. 'I don't think I should have come,' I said into the silence.

'Maybe it would have been better if you had warned them,' Hilda said gently.

I nodded. 'Yes, you are quite right. I should have done.' I wondered now why on earth I hadn't. Why in fact I had just taken if for granted that everyone would welcome me.

As if guessing my thoughts Hilda reached out and touched my arm gently. 'Don't worry, we're pleased to see you, Harry and I. Especially me,' she added with a smile.

Impulsively I jumped up and kissed her lightly on the cheek. I could feel the tears stinging my eyes; her warmth and kindness, in such contrast to my relatives, had touched me on the raw. Even as I did so I saw her stiffen and move a hand as if she wanted to ward me off; her eyes were looking beyond me to the door. I straightened, looked around and saw my Aunt Natalie standing there.

I turned and faced her. 'I — I just came to tell Hilda that I would not be in for lunch tomorrow,' I gabbled, angry with myself for feeling somehow that I had been caught out in something — I really didn't know quite what. But one glance at my aunt's face told me that she was definitely not pleased.

'There was no need,' she said coolly. 'I am here to tell her that myself.' She moved into the kitchen holding the door open as she did so in a manner that made it very plain I was expected to go through it. Unable to find an excuse to stay, I left. This time I had no hesitation but bounded up the stairs almost two at a time in my eagerness to reach the sanctuary of my own room. But once more I was foiled. Halfway up I met Nigel, apparently on his way down. As he was blocking my way I was forced to stop and ask him to please excuse me. He smiled down from two steps above me.

'Why the hurry, dear cuz?'

'The name is Maggie!' I snapped back.

He raised an eyebrow. 'You are also cousin,' he insisted. 'But you are begging the question: 'Why the hurry, Cousin Maggie?''

'No reason,' I told him. 'I just — I just . . . ' I tailed off helplessly. 'I was going to my room to — to get a handkerchief,' I finished lamely. 'Please,' I added humbly, 'may I pass now?'

He stood aside and let me pass. I managed not to look back but I had the curious feeling that he was watching me intently as I walked past Great-Aunt Sybil's door. As I reached my own door I heard him continue down the stairs. I doubled back and tapped sharply on the heavy polished panels of the old lady's room and was rewarded by an instant 'Come in!'

I didn't quite know what had made me act on this impulse, possibly two things; from my great-aunt I had received a welcome, at least I was sure there was no antipathy there, it was the same craving for acceptance, if not affection that had drawn me to the kitchen earlier. The other reason was a strange reluctance to let Nigel see me go in.

She was still sitting in the chair by the window. 'Ah, child!' She held out her hand to me. 'I'm glad to see you!'

I hurried across the room and took her outstretched hand, some sixth sense telling me what she needed. 'Shall I help you back to bed?'

'Please!' She gripped my fingers and with her other hand on the arm of the chair pulled herself to her feet. I soon had her settled and comfortable in her bed again. She thanked me as I fluffed up the pillows. 'You are quite expert.' She commented.

'I've had practice,' I told her, remembering those last weeks Mum had been at home.

She just patted my hand, but I knew that she understood what I was saying. This was the only one of my family with whom I really felt any rapport.

'I think I have been a foolish old woman,' she surprised me by saying. 'Shutting myself away like this. I intend to change now you are here. I shall get up a little each day in my room until I feel strong enough to come downstairs. You will help me?' It was a plea more than a question but before I could reply she went on: 'And please — I would prefer it if you didn't mention it to anyone else. I — I would like to — surprise them.'

'Of course I will help you!' Then I remembered. 'Only, well . . . tomorrow I shan't be here. I'm going out for the day,' I told her. I tried to keep the pleasure out of my voice and sound regretful but I don't think I succeeded.

'Out? With — with one of the family?' Her eyes were keen and her voice had a sharp ring.

I shook my head. 'No. With . . . with a friend. Someone from Australia,' I told her.

She leaned back on the cushions with a sigh of what sounded like relief. 'Ahh, I see.' She looked at me keenly for a moment then asked, just as Nigel had a short while earlier, 'Someone special — boyfriend perhaps?'

I shook my head. 'Just a friend,' I assured her.

She reached out and took one of my hands in her own. 'I'm so glad you have a friend here. I would not like to think you were quite alone.'

I wanted to tell her about Tim, just explain how normal he was, but I could not find the words without seeming to compare him with my family (to their detriment) of which, after all, she was also a member. So I just smiled and told her I was sorry I would not be here to help her tomorrow, but perhaps I could when I got back?

She nodded. 'Don't concern yourself, my dear. Hilda will give me any assistance I need, I am sure, and when you get back be sure to come and see me.'

I promised her I would. Then, as she seemed tired, I bade her goodnight and left her to go to my own room.

The following morning I was rummaging through my limited wardrobe, searching for clothes that would be both warm and becoming, when there was a tap on my door. I was surprised to see Hilda there when I went to open it.

'Your aunt — your Great-Aunt Sybil would like to see you if you can spare a moment before you go,' she told me.

I was ready, bundled up in my warmest sweaters, long before Tim could reasonably be expected to arrive for me. I told myself that I was ready early so that I would have plenty of time to visit with my aunt before I left. I tried to ignore the flutter of excited anticipation I was feeling at the prospect of seeing Tim again.

Great-Aunt Sybil, to my surprise, was standing in the middle of the room when I opened the door. The white knuckles of her hand clutching the handle of her stick betrayed her reliance on it; nevertheless she stood tall and erect with no other sign of weakness. I resisted the temptation to rush forward and help her, sensing that this would not be appreciated.

'You are standing up!' I stated the obvious and cursed my banality.

'I am!' she replied. 'But to tell the truth I'm a little more tottery than I expected. 'The spirit is willing, but the flesh . . . '' she quoted with a rueful smile. 'Perhaps you would help me to my chair?'

I swiftly crossed the room to her side. But when I tried to support her she gave an impatient shrug. 'Just walk with me — be ready to catch me.' She sighed as she dropped into the comfortable armchair in the big bay window. 'Now, not a word to anyone that I am capable of getting on my feet,' she commanded. 'With a little practice I shall soon be able to walk downstairs; that will surprise everyone!' Her voice rang with grim satisfaction at the thought. 'Now, my dear, you go out and enjoy yourself!'

'I'll certainly try!' I assured her.

Great-Aunt Sybil nodded and held up one

well-manicured hand in a curiously commanding gesture. Her voice when she spoke was level without any particular expression or emphasis; it was this I think that had more impact on me than anything.

'If you decide not to come back, I shall understand. I shall be sorry, for myself, but I shall understand. Just think of yourself, my dear.'

'But of course I shall be back!' I protested. 'Why on earth shouldn't I? I'm only going out for the day!'

Once more she held up her hand. She was, I thought, a very regal old lady yet the emotion she inspired in me was affection and pity. Certainly not fear. Impulsively I dropped to my knees by her chair and took her hands in my own.

'Where else would I go? This is my family.' In my rush of emotion engendered by the way she had touched my heartstrings so unexpectedly I forgot that they were a family I had barely known even existed a short time ago and that any warm family feeling there only came from my side and not theirs. 'Of course I will be back,' I told her, embarrassed by my own emotional outburst.

She looked at me long and hard. The expression in her eyes was unfathomable. Then she nodded, withdrew her hands from mine and said briskly, 'You'd better run along now, you don't want to keep that young man of yours waiting when he arrives, do you?'

I wanted to tell her that he was not 'my young man' but her words filled me with a warm little glow that I had no wish to lose. So I just smiled, kissed her lightly on the cheek as I rose to my feet and with a cheerful, 'See you later!' I made for the door.

I hurried to my room, grabbed scarf, gloves and camera and took a quick peek in the mirror before heading down to the hall to wait for Tim. As I burst out of my room I all but collided with Nigel who appeared to have been standing just outside the door.

'Oh!' He seemed nonplussed to see me dressed in outdoor things. 'You're going out already!' It sounded like an accusation.

'Yes. My friend is picking me up.' I found myself gabbling almost guiltily and immediately felt annoyed with myself. I'd already told everyone of my plans the day before. 'Excuse me.' He was standing directly in front of me so that short of actually pushing him out of the way I could not reach the stairs.

'Shall you be out all day?' he asked, keeping step with me on the wide staircase.

I nodded, willing him to stop quizzing me. But even as his mouth was opening to ask me the next question we both froze in our tracks as a scream from the kitchen region reverberated through the house. We both quickly unfroze and headed toward the sound. As I hurtled up the passage to the kitchen I heard the front doorbell clanging. For the briefest of seconds I hesitated, torn between the need to open the door to what must be Tim, and the hysterical sobs coming from the kitchen. It was, I realized, Hilda who was weeping so wildly and the rumbling undertone was Mr Ingram endeavouring to comfort her.

Hilda was rocking backwards and forwards in the old wooden rocker, her beloved ginger cat on her lap; she seemed to be making no attempt to check the tears coursing down her cheeks and ignored the large white handkerchief being proffered by her husband.

'Hilda! — Whatever . . . ?' The words died on my lips as I reached her side and saw that Marmalade was not, as I had first thought, just resting on her lap but was quite obviously dead. I stood for a moment looking down at the once proud animal. His eyes were open and staring and his lips were curled back in a snarl of frozen agony. Hilda's hands were on the body, her fingers twisting convulsively in the once luxuriant red fur.

Slowly I turned my eyes to Harry Ingram. 'What . . . ?' I began in a voice that sounded as if it belonged to someone else. I cleared my throat and began again. 'What happened?'

'Hilda thought he looked odd. She said, 'There is something wrong with Marmalade', picked him up and sat down in the chair with him. Almost immediately he let out a terrible yowl, like something in torment, went into a sort of spasm and died, right there, in her lap.' He shook his head as if in sorrowful disbelief. 'She thought the world of that cat.'

I put my arms round her still shaking shoulders and hugged her. I could guess what a shock it must have been. I had been pretty shocked myself just seeing him lying there like that, and I hadn't the emotional attachment to him that she had. I felt her relax slightly and reaching for Mr Ingram's hanky I dabbed at her face myself. 'I think a cup of tea is what you need.' I suggested.

Looking towards the door as Mr Ingram moved across my line of vision to place the singing kettle on to the hot spot of the Aga I saw Nigel crossing the kitchen followed by Tim. Dear God, in the drama of the last few moments I had quite forgotten him and certainly had never given a thought to the fact that I had left Nigel — of all people — to answer the door to him.

We managed to calm Hilda somewhat with strong tea and gentle words. Mr Ingram, and, rather to my surprise, Nigel, offered to take poor Marmalade and give him a decent burial. I found myself softening somewhat towards my cousin, maybe he wasn't so bad after all, but I did wonder just how anyone could bury anything in the present ice-bound earth. However, the problem didn't arise for Hilda stubbornly insisted that he had been perfectly fit less than an hour ago and she wanted to know how he had died so suddenly. In vain her husband and Nigel pointed out to her that he was dead, and knowing how would not bring him back.

'I want to know,' she repeated.

So it was that when Tim and I finally left together we took with us Marmalade's body that Hilda had laid tenderly in an old apple box and covered with a yellow duster. As he was placed on the back seat of the car and Mr Ingram gently but firmly drew Hilda back and closed the door, we assured her we would go immediately to the vet's surgery and leave him there with a request for an autopsy.

It was not quite how I had visualized my reunion with Tim.

6

We were out on the road and heading well away from Elwood Hall before either of us spoke. I guess the small corpse laid out on the back seat had a somewhat dampening effect on both of us. For my part I was wondering whether the bloodcurdling scream I had heard could have been Marmalade in his death agony and not — as I had first thought — Hilda. I glanced sideways at Tim; his face was set in hard lines, his hands gripped the steering wheel and his eyes were fixed on the road ahead. I was not sure whether all his attention was on negotiating the ice and snow-bound roads, so different from the dusty roads of our sun-baked homeland, or whether his thoughts were occupied with something else. I hoped the unfortunate start to the day was not causing him to regret coming to see me.

So lost in my own thoughts was I that I did not catch what he said when he did speak and had to ask him to repeat himself. 'The cat,' he said. 'I was talking about the cat. I can tell you what the vet will say even before he does an autopsy.' As his eyes did not leave the road ahead he gave the impression of talking more to himself than me. Even so I felt the need to put something into the pause.

'Oh?' I murmured encouragingly.

'Poison,' he said, 'The cat was poisoned.' This time he did glance briefly in my direction.

'Poisoned!' I echoed. 'Are you sure? How do you know?'

'I've seen other cats that have died like that — with that terrible sort of snarl on their faces. It's always been poison,' he told me.

'But that's terrible,' I cried. 'That's murder!' I was outraged. Why should anyone want to hurt poor old Marmalade who never did a thing to harm anyone, who, in fact, never did much more than doze and eat, basking all the while in the physical warmth of the kitchen and the emotional warmth of Hilda's affection for him? Sudden tears pricked my eyes as I thought of the old woman and what this must mean to her.

The grim lines on Tim's face relaxed slightly at my outburst. 'I suppose it is,' he conceded, 'though it's not a word we usually connect with animals — whatever we do to them. If I'm right and he has been poisoned then there is always the possibility — or probability — that he wasn't the intended target.'

'You mean . . . ' I said, buying into his line of thought, 'that whoever mur — did this thing was deliberately trying to hurt Hilda?'

'Either that, or the poison was meant for someone else. Now, where did they say this vet hung out?'

We were by now driving into the outskirts of Stafford. I repeated the directions that Mr Ingram had given me and we were soon, to my secret relief, handing over our dismal burden. I gave instructions for the results of the autopsy to be phoned through to the Ingrams and left the vet's surgery with a slightly lighter step determined to put the events of the morning behind me and make the most of my day out with Tim.

He obviously had much the same idea for as I settled back into the passenger seat beside him he turned to me with a smile. 'I think we need something to chase the blues away. There is an excellent pub in the centre of the town, The Swan, older than anything you will ever find back home, one of the many places I am sure where Queen Elizabeth 1st spent the night.' He chuckled, 'If you are to believe the guide books that woman can never have spent a night in her own bed!'

I had never even imagined anything as old as the pub he took me to. We parked at the rear and he led the way in through the back entrance. I was fascinated by it all, even the well worn and uneven brick flooring as I followed him to a dimly lit, fuggily warm bar with the walls decorated, like my grandfather's home, with old hunting prints. I walked across to the coal fire holding my hands out thankfully to the blaze while Tim ordered drinks.

I smiled my thanks at him over the rim of the glass feeling the froth on the beer he had ordered for us both tickling my top lip.

'No wonder they don't go in for chilled beer,' I remarked. 'Who would want it in this weather?' I looked round me appreciatively as my eyes grew accustomed to the dim lighting. 'You seem to know your way around here,' I commented, remembering how he had brought me in through the rear entrance.

Tim nodded. 'I stayed here last night.'

'Oh.' Why did I feel such a stab of disappointment to learn that he had actually been in Stafford since yesterday. Surely I hadn't thought he had come all the way from London just to see me? He'd told me he'd had an assignment.

'I decided to come up yesterday so that I would be free to entertain you today. I did most of my work last night.' He smiled at me as he put his now empty glass down on the table. 'Drink up and I'll show you a few sights, then we'll come back here for lunch.'

Obediently I drained my glass.

'There is a bit of an old ruined castle just out of town,' he told me. 'Something else you won't see back in Oz. I need to get some pictures of it. You've got your camera I suppose?' I nodded and patted the bag over my shoulder.

Even though I had seen plenty of pictures of old castles the reality of what was, as he said, only the ruined remains of one, made me realize how much age and history there was in this country. As I looked up at the old grey stone I suddenly felt very insignificant in the great scheme of things. I was not sorry when Tim suggested a walk round the town before lunch.

It seemed to me as we pressed our way through the crowds on the pavements that everything was smaller and much more crowded than the towns back home. Having had little opportunity to use it I still found the currency confusing and Tim reminded me more than once that dollars and pounds did not have the same value and obligingly told me what the same items would cost back in Australia. Expensive or not I decided I would have to buy a decent pair of boots if I was to walk out much in the snow. Snow which here in the town was unpleasant grey slush, and very wet indeed.

I looked up at the sign swinging over the pub as we made our way back in, this time through the front door. Absurdly I was surprised to see the swan was white. Tim followed my gaze. 'You didn't expect a black one did you?' he teased.

The dining-room, like everywhere else it seemed, was crowded. Tim had had the foresight to book a table for two and we had been placed in a warm corner close to another blazing fire. I pulled off my gloves and slipped out of my parka and smiled across the table at my companion. He was studying the menu so I was able to study him. Yes, I thought, he really was as attractive as I had remembered him. Looking up he met my gaze.

'Have you decided?'

I shook my head. 'Er, no.' I hadn't even glanced at the menu although it was in my hand.

After some consultation we both decided to have a thoroughly British meal of soup, roast beef and Yorkshire pudding followed by apple pie. By the time we reached the coffee stage I was feeling as if I would never waddle out of the place, not to mention a certain light-headedness from the second beer we had with the meal. English beer must be stronger than Australian beer I decided.

'How long are you planning to stay with your family?' he asked me.

'I don't know,' I admitted, wondering as I spoke if I really wanted to stay with them at all.

'They sound a little — odd.'

'Yes — I suppose they are. But do you know,' I confessed 'my Great-Aunt Sybil who is definitely about the oddest of them all is the one I feel closest to?' I shrugged. 'Maybe that means I am a little odd too!'

'What about that cousin of yours — the one I met this morning?'

'Nigel? Well, yes, I suppose he's all right. I mean he has been quite nice to me,' I admitted. 'Well, to be honest no one has been nasty, except ... ' I tailed off, somehow unwilling to admit that my own grandfather had more or less refused to acknowledge my existence.

'Except?' Tim prompted.

'Well, I haven't actually spoken to my grandfather,' I told him.

Tim was not going to let me off the hook. 'What exactly do you mean you haven't spoken to him? It must be a bit difficult staying in the same house!'

'It isn't my fault!' I imagined he was being

critical. 'I tried to introduce myself to him and he simply said he knew who I was and wheeled himself off to his own room and I haven't seen him since.'

'Wheeled himself off?'

'Yes, he is a cripple in a wheelchair. A hunting accident,' I explained. My throat felt tight, I hadn't realized, or admitted to myself, how my grandfather's behaviour had hurt me until I had to talk about it.

Tim looked at me across the table, his eyes keen but not critical. 'How odd,' he remarked before raising his coffee cup to his lips and draining it.

'Yes,' I murmured bleakly before prattling on about my great-aunt and her parrot. 'He is a Sulphur Crested Cockatoo called Ozzie, so at least I have a compatriot in the house.' I smiled brightly, hoping that my words did not reveal the loneliness my family home so often made me feel which in itself brought with it an ache of longing for Australia where, at this time of the year, it would still be high summer. But thinking of my homeland brought in its train memories of my mother and the sharp realization that the only family I had were here. I realized that Tim was looking round for the waitress to collect the bill.

'I'm sorry Maggie. But I'm afraid I have to get back to London. That means I am going to have to take you back to the bosom of your family and your ancestral home.'

'Oh, yes — of course.' I began to gather up my gloves and bag and look around for my parka over the back of the chair. Why had I thought that our outing would be more prolonged?

Suddenly he leaned across the table towards me. 'You do want to go back, don't you?' he asked.

I stared at him. What did he mean? What was he talking about?

'You don't have to, you know. You could — well, you could come back to London with me.'

I shook my head slowly. 'I can't just walk out. I am expected back,' I told him. Yet even as I spoke I remembered my aunt suggesting I might prefer not to. For a moment I was tempted. Then I thought of her relying on me to help her give up her lonely bed-ridden existence. I thought of poor Hilda who had lost her cat. I knew that, like it or not, I was involved with these people and I must return — for the time being at least.

'Will you come in?' I asked Tim as he drew up outside the imposing front door of Elwood Hall.

He shook his head. 'Not this time, Maggie. I do really have to get back to London and I can't say I like the look of the weather. By the look of that sky we could even have more snow.'

I was disappointed, but he had said 'not this time'. 'You — you'll come again?' I asked hesitantly.

For a moment our eyes held. 'I'll come again,' he said. For me that was enough. Even as he spoke his eyes changed focus to look beyond me towards the house. 'You have a welcoming committee of one,' he remarked drily, but before I could turn my head he leaned towards me and kissed me lightly on the cheek. 'Take care! And don't forget — you have my number.' With that he revved up the engine and I had no choice but to get out of the car. As I did so I saw my cousin Nigel standing in the open front door. I slammed the car door shut, stepped back and raised my hand in a farewell salute to Tim. Only as the car disappeared from view did I turn slowly and mount the steps to the front door. Was it, I wondered, in spite of or because Nigel waited for me that I felt such reluctance to enter the house. I raised my head and pasted a bright smile on my face as I reached the top step.

'Thanks!' I said as I passed him to go into the house. 'I hope you haven't let too much cold air in.'

Nigel ignored my rather facetious remark and ushered me in the direction of the lounge where, to my relief, a fire burned brightly. The twins who had a small table between them and were engrossed in what appeared to be a very large jigsaw however took most of the heat.

'Had a nice day with your boyfriend?' One of them, I had no idea which, asked without even bothering to look up. I was about to deny this description of Tim then I thought, What the heck! Let them think what they like. After all, it could certainly do no harm to my standing and might even be a deterrent to any unwelcome attentions from my cousin, if they all thought there was more in my relationship with Tim than there was in reality.

'Do you think we will get any afternoon tea today?' one of the twins asked.

The other shrugged. 'May have to get it ourselves. If Hilda isn't capable yet.'

'If you want any that's a good suggestion,' Nigel commented.

Neither girl made any offer to move, and realizing that if they did I would probably be left cosily alone with Nigel, I promptly offered to go to the kitchen myself. I was already at the door when Nigel began to protest. I was certainly not in the least hungry after the enormous lunch I had enjoyed with

Tim but I did want to see how Hilda was bearing up and if she had any news yet from the vet's surgery.

I found her listlessly buttering scones; the tea trolley was already laid. 'I came to help you,' I told her 'And to see if you had heard anything?'

She shook her head. 'Not yet. Anyway, what does it matter? He's dead isn't he? Harry is right — knowing how he died won't bring him back.' She put the plate of scones down on the trolley alongside an appetizing cherry cake, and turned to the Aga to pour the boiling water into the teapot. Her mouth was set in a thin line and I guessed she did not want to talk about Marmalade. Silence, heavy and oppressive hung over the kitchen, only punctuated by a loud snore from Sadie as she snoozed away in the warmth from the stove. I was almost glad to take charge of the trolley and head back for the lounge. As I moved towards the door I noticed a couple of trays also laid for afternoon tea. One I guessed was for my grandfather and the other probably for my great-aunt.

'I had such a huge lunch I don't really want anything.' I told Hilda. 'Though a cup of tea might be nice. I think I will put an extra cup on Great-Aunt Sybil's tray and have one with her, so I will take her tray up for you.'

'Thank you!' Hilda seemed grateful to be spared the trip up the stairs. 'I can squeeze it on the trolley and you can leave that for the others then take hers up.' She was putting the extra cup and saucer on the tray as she spoke.

I delivered the trolley, then picking up the tray left the room murmuring that I was taking my great-aunt's tray up. I found Great-Aunt Sybil once more seated in the window. She had a small table in front of her and was, I thought, playing patience. But when I got close to her I saw that the cards she had laid out in front of her were not the standard pack but brightly coloured tarot cards. Unwilling to disturb her I pulled up another small table and placed the tray on it. She looked up and smiled her thanks.

'Good. I see you have brought two cups — that means you are going to stay and tell me about your day!' As she spoke she swept the cards to one side, tapped them into a neat pack and began to roll them up in a lavender-coloured silk scarf that was lying in her lap. This done she put them in a beautifully carved wooden box and snapped the lid shut with an air of dismissal.

'I want to hear how you enjoyed yourself,' She told me, 'but first can you tell me why there is a black cloud over the house? More so than usual, that is. I can feel it, but no one has explained it to me. It seems to centre around Hilda.'

I looked directly at the old lady and meeting those piercing eyes knew that I had no alternative but to tell her the truth.

'Marmalade died this morning.'

'Marmalade, Hilda's cat? But she adored him — she must be devastated,' she exclaimed. 'How? What happened? Had he been sick? Was he run over?'

'He — he just died,' I told her rather lamely. But she wasn't satisfied with this.

'Things don't 'just die'!' she retorted with some asperity. 'There has to be a reason.'

'I'm telling you the truth. He did just die. But because Hilda, like you, thought there had to be a reason Tim and I took him into the vet this morning for an autopsy.'

'And?' she prompted.

I shook my head. 'We haven't heard the result yet but . . . ' I was about to pass on Tim's opinion but, unwilling to upset her, decided to hold my tongue. Great-Aunt Sybil however had heard that 'but'.

'You're not telling me everything,' she accused.

I smiled slightly at her perspicacity. 'Well,' I admitted, 'Tim thinks he was poisoned.'

'Oh dear! Poor Hilda! That is dreadful for her. But who on earth would do a thing like that? And why?' she mused. I saw her shoot a glance at Ozzie on his perch, for once fairly quiet and apparently taking in the conversation. 'I know how I should feel if it were Ozzie!'

The thought that Marmalade might not be the only victim had not crossed my mind before. Now I, too, looked at the parrot for whom I had a soft spot for, as I had said to Tim, he was a compatriot after all. Then my thoughts flew to Sadie, dear, kind, fat, greedy old Sadie, eminently lovable and harmless. Suppose the same thing happened to her?

'Pour the tea, would you, dear?' I was brought back by my great-aunt's request. As I passed her cup to her I saw that her features were set in a stern mould but that she had no intention of discussing this unhappy circumstance any further. Instead, she asked me again about my day.

I told her how Tim had taken me to see the ruins of the old castle and how — as a complete contrast — we had then walked round the town and I had bought myself a strong pair of boots so that I could walk in the snow, and about our lunch at The Swan.

'And what did you think of our town?' she asked me.

'Very crowded!' I told her. 'Or so it seemed to me after Australian towns. There seemed a lot more people and a lot less space. But the shops' I added, in case she should think me carping, 'are excellent, though things did seem expensive to me compared with home. I loved the pub. So incredibly old. Tim said Queen Elizabeth 1st probably slept there!' I laughed, but she answered me seriously. 'She probably did. Certainly quite a lot of famous people have stayed there down the centuries. Did you have a good lunch?'

I nodded. 'Terrific, which is why I can only drink a cup of tea now!' I told her as I passed her the scones. In the silence that followed I nodded towards the carved box that contained the tarot cards. 'My mother had tarot cards,' I told her.

'Ah, she kept them, did she? Did she use them?'

'A little, she used them for herself and occasionally read for friends,' I told her. 'But she would never read for me. She said 'never for one's nearest and dearest'.'

Great-Aunt Sybil nodded. 'I told her that. When I gave her the cards and taught her to read them. Did she teach you?'

I shook my head. 'Not really. She always said she would one day, but, well, I guess that day never came,' I finished sadly.

Resolutely I pushed sad thoughts of what

might have been to one side.

'I'll teach you, if you like. If you stay here long enough!'

'Thank you.' I was not at all sure I wanted to stay in this household long enough to learn. However, there were other things to think about at the moment.

'Now,' Great-Aunt Sybil said pushing away her teacup. 'I want you to help me. I intend to come downstairs for dinner tonight. But I shall need your help. When you take my tray to the kitchen will you tell Hilda that I shall be down. If I take my time I can get dressed on my own but I shall need a strong young arm, yours my dear, to help me down those stairs.'

'Are you sure?' I asked her, meaning was she sure she wanted to come downstairs for dinner.

'I'm sure,' she told me. 'I shall expect you at 6.30 this evening.'

When I delivered her tray and her message to Hilda in the kitchen the latter gave a 'tcch' of irritation. 'What would she want to be coming down for today?' she demanded. 'I haven't the time to help her.'

'Oh, don't worry about that, Hilda. She has asked me to help her down the stairs. She assures me she can get herself dressed and ready.'

'No doubt she can! I'm just hoping she won't be causing trouble when she gets down.' Hilda heaved a deep sigh. 'There has been enough of that already for one day.'

'Yes,' I agreed. As I was speaking the phone could be heard ringing in the hall. As if in silent agreement both of us held our breath and waited. A few minutes later Mr Ingram returned to the kitchen. One look at his face and I guessed we had been right — the phone call had been from the vet's surgery. His expression was bleak.

Hilda gave another exclamation of irritation and impatience. 'Was that about Marmalade?' Her voice was sharp. I, too, felt a strong urge to shake the news out of the old man myself.

Slowly he nodded. 'Yes. It would seem — well, they say he was quite definitely poisoned.' His eyes were on his wife's face and he seemed scarcely able to tell her. But if he had been expecting some sort of an outburst, of grief or anger or simple disbelief he should have been relieved. Slowly the colour seemed to drain from Hilda's face; she reached one hand out for the kitchen table to steady herself.

'I knew it!' Her voice was little more than a whisper. 'But who, in this house, would stoop to such a cruel thing? Dear God — my poor

Marmalade!' Slowly the colour came back into her cheeks but at the same time her lip trembled and her eyes filled. She groped in her pocket for her handkerchief and firmly, but with a wonderful tenderness, Harry Ingram pushed her gently down into a chair. He then turned to the dresser, opened a cupboard and drew out a bottle of brandy.

'I think she needs a snifter,' he told me with a wry smile as he poured some of the fiery liquid into a glass and handed it to her. He obviously understood her well for after an initial gasp as she took her first sip Hilda seemed to pull herself together as each drop passed her lips.

By the time the glass was empty she got up from the chair, twitched her apron straight, looked us both firmly in the eyes and with a visible squaring of her shoulders said, 'Well, this won't do. I can't sit here feeling sorry for myself or moping. I have a dinner to cook!' It was clear that as far as she was concerned the subject of her cat and his unhappy end was now taboo.

I smiled at Harry then said to her back as she busied herself with something on the stove, 'Don't worry about Great-Aunt Sybil, I will see she gets downstairs safely. That is if she still wants to.' Then I turned on my heel and left the kitchen.

Hilda may have put the matter of her cat's poisoning to the back of her mind but I couldn't. Tim had raised too many questions for that.

7

I presented myself at my great-aunt's door punctually; in fact the grandfather clock down in the hall began to strike the half hour as I turned the door knob.

She was, as she had promised, ready and still looked quite imposing too. Her silver-blue hair shone in the light with an almost iridescent sheen and she was well made up. Her hands, which bore at least one ring on every finger, were tipped with scarlet nails. She was seated in her chair with one hand already resting on the silver head of her ebony cane, around her shoulders was a pure silk shawl, heavily tasselled, with a black background shot through with jewel colours. Beneath it she wore a long black dress. Even though I had by now come to accept her somewhat bizarre appearance as normal I must have registered my surprise for she smiled with a sort of grim satisfaction as she gestured to me to help her to her feet.

'They all think I am a witch,' she commented. 'So I wouldn't like to disappoint them by appearing dull.'

'Great-Aunt Sybil, you could never appear

dull,' I assured her as I helped her to her feet.

Slowly we made a sort of majestic descent down the wide staircase. She gave me her cane to hold in my left hand for her own right one was fully occupied with the banister. Her other hand clutched my right arm in a vice-like grip that almost made me wince. But we made it, and once in the hall she paused, took a deep breath, took her cane from me and made a slow but dignified and unaided progress towards the dining-room.

We were the first there and I realized that this was what she had intended when she commanded my presence in her room at 6.30, for dinner was seldom served before 7 p.m. I saw her eyes quickly rake the table covered in white linen and gleaming silver and guessed she was counting the places and checking to see if she had, in fact, been laid for. I wondered where she would sit.

She took the place at one end of the long table normally occupied by Gerald. The other end was, as usual, placeless for my grandfather had not joined in a meal since I had been in the house. As she sat down she turned to me. 'Would you mind going to the kitchen and asking Harry to set another place and to tell my brother that he is expected in the dining-room tonight. If I can manage to walk down the stairs then he can wheel himself in here.'

I must have looked a bit stupefied for she waved a hand at me in a gesture that was both dismissive and authoritative.

'Go along child, before they all troop in,' she instructed, adding, with a wicked gleam of amusement, 'If you don't want to go all the way to the kitchen you can always deliver the message to your grandfather yourself.'

I hastened to the kitchen. Both Ingrams were fully occupied with the last minute preparations for the meal but muttering something to himself Mr Ingram complied with my great-aunt's request. For my part I wished that I could stay here and have my dinner with the Ingrams.

As I made my way back through the hall I could hear my grandfather shouting at Mr Ingram. I thought he sounded very angry. I had barely reached the dining-room when he wheeled himself in.

'What the devil is all this, Sybil?' he demanded. 'Why can't I have my dinner in peace without being bothered with relations from all over the world?' This was obviously an allusion to me and, as I was undoubtedly meant to, I felt angry and hurt and bridled in response to his words.

'You may certainly have your dinner in

peace, Grandfather,' I told him, stressing the last word. 'I will have mine elsewhere.'

'Sit down and don't be such a fool, Maggie!' Aunt Sybil snapped. 'And as for you, Adrian, you will stop being a fool too. What is past is past. What happened between you and Angela is nothing to do with this child; nothing whatsoever, and I should have thought you would have had more sense. Take your place at the head of the table before they all come in. And you, Maggie,' she turned her gaze on me, 'sit down too, wherever you usually sit.'

We both did as we were told, and if I was surprised at myself for capitulating so easily I was totally amazed to see my formidable and irascible old grandfather meekly wheel his chair to the head of the table where a place had now been set for him.

So it was that when the rest of the family straggled into dinner a few minutes later the three of us were already seated. I watched the varying expressions cross their faces as they came in, ranging from mere surprise through astonishment to downright dismay. A dull flush suffused my Uncle Gerald's face when he saw that his usual place at one end of the table had been taken by Great-Aunt Sybil, but though I am sure he thought plenty, he said nothing. Only Nigel seemed pleased and greeted both old people pleasantly. As I watched, he shot me a swift smile in which I thought I detected a gleam of triumph, or was it malice? I lowered my gaze and picking up my table napkin concentrated on spreading it neatly on my lap. Raising my eyes and looking round the table I thought that I had never known a family in which so many undercurrents seemed to ebb and flow. But then, of course, ever since I could remember, my family had been just my mother and myself.

Conversation was stilted and paltry during the meal. Jackie and Josie were chattering together speculating on who could have killed Marmalade — and why. Sophie, who had struck me on my arrival as being one of the more kind-hearted of my relatives, endeavoured to shush them, no doubt partly out of consideration for the Ingrams and partly because she obviously did not consider it a 'nice' subject for the dinner table. She had little success, fifteen-year-old girls not being known for their deference to their mother's views. Their father, Gerald, appeared to be sulking about the loss of his position at the end of the table.

His sister, Natalie, on the other hand could not have been more solicitous of their father, my grandfather. In fact I could almost say she was positively grovelling. He, for his part, steadfastly ignored her; as he did everyone else at the table. My great-aunt appeared to have used up her energy just making it to the table and had none left for conversation. I, too, would have given my attention to my food and my own thoughts had not Nigel drawn me inexorably into a conversation with him. I had to admit that of the entire family he seemed the only one to have any knowledge of, and interest in, Australia. Perhaps it was because I had been with Tim, or maybe it was just that, family or not. I felt very much the alien in their midst. Whatever it was I was only too happy to talk of Australia. After a while the twins, having exhausted the possibilities and speculations about poor Marmalade began to join in. Though their participation could scarcely be called intelligent. It seemed to me they were vying with each other to sound stupid themselves and make me look it too by the inane questions they asked me.

When, in response to a comment that Nigel made, I said that the traffic seemed very dense and the roads very narrow here compared to my home town, one of them remarked that they supposed cars were pretty rare in Australia. I was goaded to respond by saying somewhat acidly, 'Yes, you would like it in Australia as you are so fond of horses for we are still back in the horse and buggy days down there.' I could see by their expressions that they were not sure whether I was serious or taking the mickey out of them.

Nigel had no such doubts. 'Bravo, Maggie; definitely one up to you there!'

I turned to smile at him and doing so caught my grandfather watching me keenly, and if I was not mistaken the gleam in his eye was one of approval. But if I expected my approval rating to rise with the girls I was sadly disappointed. I had made them look foolish; from the surly looks that passed between them I didn't think they would forgive me in a hurry.

What seemed an interminable meal eventually dragged to a close. Curtly declining coffee my grandfather pushed back from the table, wheeled himself briskly out of the room, and presumably back to his own quarters.

I looked at my great-aunt; her face under its mask of heavy make-up looked drawn and her eyes seemed to have lost their fire. She turned to me but before she could ask I leaned towards her and asked, 'Shall I help you up the stairs, Great-Aunt Sybil?'

Her eyes lit with gratitude. 'Thank you, my dear. I should be grateful!' The lack of hauteur told me how tired she was. As I went to help her up from her chair she stumbled and almost fell. Instantly Nigel was on the other side of her giving her a strong arm to lean on.

'Let me, Aunt.' He was all solicitude, and in the event it was Nigel who almost carried her up the stairs and all I did was bring up the rear with her cane in my hand.

When we reached the haven of her room at last she smiled at us both. 'Thank you!' she said to Nigel. 'Goodnight!' Thus dismissed he had little alternative but to bid her a goodnight and go back downstairs. My aunt turned with her hand on the door knob of her room. 'Could I . . . would it be too much to ask you to help me to bed, my dear?'

'Of course!' I assured her, wishing that I had offered before I had been asked.

By the time I had her settled amongst her pillows I, too, was feeling totally exhausted.

'Thank you, my dear. Tomorrow I shall — I hope — be a little more in training, a little more able to do things for myself.' She smiled and patted my hand. Impulsively I leaned down and kissed the parchment cheek.

'I'm sure you will!' I told her. Straightening up I stifled a yawn. 'I'm feeling pretty tired myself — I think I shall turn in,' I said.

I was at the door when she called me. 'Maggie, do you think I am a wicked old witch?' she asked.

Surprised I smiled back at her. 'A witch, perhaps — wicked, no!'

Her chortle of delight sounded very witchlike to me as I once more bade her goodnight and closed the door.

In spite of the fact that I was, as I had claimed, tired, sleep did not come easily to me. I tossed and turned mulling over the events of the day. There was plenty to occupy my mind. First the trauma of poor Marmalade's death, which I still thought of as murder. Also on the minus side the uncomfortable atmosphere at the dinner table tonight. There had certainly been no warm welcome for my great-aunt on her return to the family table. As my thoughts wandered around that table remembering each person in turn it suddenly occurred to me that of them all I was only actually related by blood to two of them, my grandfather and Great-Aunt Sybil. Somehow it was a cheering thought!

Finally, before sleep claimed me at last, I thought of Tim; the more I saw of him the more I liked him. I hoped he felt the same way.

I do not know what woke me with such a start. I cannot believe that I was sleeping so lightly that the faint squeak of my bedroom door handle turning could have roused me.

Whatever it was I sat up suddenly in bed, uncomfortably aware of the thudding of my own heart, and blindly groped for the switch of the bedside light. As its welcome beam flooded the room I distinctly saw the knob on my bedroom door turning and heard the sound, soft but distinct, of the door closing.

Without stopping to think I leapt out of bed and flung open the door. There was nothing there but the inky darkness of a moonless mid-winter night at three in the morning. I checked the time when I returned to bed. I peered uselessly into the darkness, suddenly aware that it was not only dark but also very cold and I was clad only in my night clothes. A shiver shook my frame, how much of it was induced by cold and how much by fear I do not know. It was certainly fear as much as anything that sent me spinning back to my bed, for as I stood there I heard, quite distinctly, over and above the sound of my own breathing, the soft, infinitely sinister, sound of another breath.

For a moment I crouched on the bed with my knees pulled up and my arms wrapped tightly around them, my eyes fixed unblinkingly on that door knob watching and waiting for it to turn again. Yet another shiver ran down my spine and my eyes began to water with the strain until some remnant of common sense came to my aid. I could not, I realized, spend the rest of the night like this. Or if I did I would almost certainly be frozen stiff by morning; nor could I possibly lie down and go to sleep with the knowledge that someone was out there. Someone who had been about to enter my room. For what purpose I dare not even hazard a guess.

Without taking my eyes from the door I slid off the bed, pushed my feet into my slippers and pulled my robe round my shoulders. Summoning all the courage I didn't know I possessed I crossed the room to the door, pulled a fairly heavy chair over to it and, tilting it wedged the back firmly under the knob. It was only then that I realized that the heavy, rather old-fashioned fitting could be locked — if I had the key! I returned to my bed after satisfying myself that if anyone did try and get in now at least I would hear them. I told myself that I would stay awake the rest of the night and get hold of that key tomorrow.

I woke some hours later to find the sun streaming through a chink in the curtains, the bedside light still on and a chair pushed up against the door. I knew then that I had not been dreaming. I looked at my watch; it was almost 9 o'clock. I had not only slept but I had over-slept. Not surprising, I thought, my subconscious knew best! My nose sticking out over the bedclothes told me that it was cold; the sun told me it was a bright day and helped to dispel my night-time fears. Maybe after all it had just been a dream or my waking imagination. All the same I decided to leave that chair in place until I was dressed and ready to leave my room.

Pulling on a heavy sweater I walked across to the window and drew back the curtains. There must have been a sharp frost overnight for the pane was frosted in a more intricate and delicate pattern than any human eye and hand could fashion. Where the sun struck directly it was beginning to melt very slightly. I rubbed a small patch with my finger and my sunburned soul gasped at the sheer beauty of the garden below me draped in its sparkling white mantle and glistening icicles which were now beginning to drip slightly in the sun.

I turned back into the room and walked across to the dressing table to fix my face and hair before putting in an appearance down-stairs. As I picked up my brush my hand paused in mid-air and I gave a little gasp. Lying in the middle of my dressing table was an old-fashioned door key. I picked it up and walked across to the door. Pulling the chair aside I slid it easily into the lock. It turned without complaint. I tried the knob; my door was locked. I was stupefied. I was just about one hundred per cent certain that key had not been there yesterday. But who had put it there? And why? The answer was as elusive as my unseen visitor of the night before; and almost as disturbing. I withdrew the key and slipped it, bulky as it was, into the pocket of my jeans before leaving my room to go in search of breakfast.

The house seemed strangely quiet as I made my way downstairs. I realized that the normal breakfast hour had come and gone while I slept but still I wondered just where everyone had got to. I would have made my way straight to the kitchen but as I passed the dining-room I saw that Sophie and Natalie were both still at the table. The latter was buttering toast and talking in a low voice while her sister-in-law gazed into space over the coffee cup she cradled in her hands. I hesitated and would have continued on my way to the kitchen if Sophie had not looked toward the open door at that moment and seen me.

'Good morning, Maggie!' she called brightly, at the same time shooting a warning glance at Natalie who abruptly cut short her monologue. 'Come on in and have some breakfast!'

Thus summoned I had little choice but to obey, although my appetite suddenly seemed a little less keen. I pulled a chair out and assured Sophie that, no, I did not want anything cooked. Coffee and toast would do me very well. I drew a cup towards me and helped myself to coffee from the electric percolator, aware that both women were scrutinizing me keenly. As I looked up and met their gaze across the table Sophie gave a nervous half-smile and turned away. Natalie on the other hand held my gaze and coolly inquired if I had slept well.

'Like a top!' I assured her. While at the same time I wondered why she should care. My 'sensible' self immediately supplied the answer — she didn't care. She was merely being polite. It would be foolish I told myself to get so uptight that I read hidden meaning into every remark. Nevertheless my fingers closed for a moment on the key in my pocket.

'We were discussing Marmalade,' Natalie spoke coolly. 'Of course, I am sorry about him but I do hope that Hilda will pull herself together today. She really was quite useless yesterday.'

'I can understand her being upset,' I murmured in her defence.

'Of course! But he was, after all, only a cat!'

'She was very fond of him, Nat,' Sophie remarked. Then looking across the table at me, said, 'Did you know someone had cut a bit of fur off him, isn't that odd?'

'Yes,' I agreed. Thinking it was indeed strange but Natalie cut in across my thoughts.

'That's what Hilda told you, Sophie. How she could be sure I do not know. The damn cat had so much fur, he was always losing tufts all over the place!' As she spoke she pushed her chair back from the table. 'Well, I can't sit here all day, I must go and see Hilda and discuss today's meals. You will, I take it, be here for lunch?' I realized she was speaking to me now.

I nodded. 'Yes. I — I expect so.' Unless, I thought to myself, I can find some excuse and some means to escape this house altogether and for ever.

As Natalie turned away from the table she shot a look of irritation — annoyance, warning, I couldn't be sure which — at Sophie. 'Well, I can't stay here chattering,' she remarked and left us.

I was not sorry. I never found her in any way easy to be around. I much preferred Sophie of the two. But left alone with her now I was aware of the silence hanging between us. A silence that seemed to me all too full of unspoken thoughts. As quickly as I could I finished my own coffee and got up from the table with no more meaningful conversation passing between us than a comment about the weather. As I passed the telephone in the hall I thought of Tim and, obeying a sudden impulse went to it and dialled his number. I had a good memory for things like phone numbers and had committed his to memory, maybe some instinctive feeling that I might need it in a hurry some time had prompted me. I was just about to replace the receiver as no one seemed to be answering when a woman's voice came on the line.

'No,' she told me in response to my query. 'I'm sorry but Tim is not here at the moment, would you like to leave a message?'

'No — no,' I said. 'No message.'

'Shall I tell him you rang?'

I was about to say no when I saw Nigel crossing the hall towards me. Something made me say, 'Yes, yes please. Just tell him Maggie called, will you?'

Nigel was standing close behind me when I replaced the receiver and turned round. I thought he seemed, well, annoyed was probably too strong a word — just not pleased. But the slight frown soon left his face to be replaced by a smile.

'I was looking for you,' he told me. 'Where have you been? I have to go to Birmingham

119

for the day on business. I thought you might like to come with me?'

I hesitated for a fraction of a second. The prospect of a day out away from this house and all its undercurrents was more than pleasing. If Nigel had business to attend to I would not have to spend all the time with him. 'I'd love to!' I told him. 'I'll dash up and get my outdoor things. Oh . . . ' I paused with my foot already on the bottom step. 'I'd better tell Hilda I won't be in for lunch after all. I told your mother I would be. And I'll just pop in to tell Great-Aunt Sybil I am going out.'

'I'll tell Hilda,' he assured me. 'And there is no need to waste time telling old Sybil. She isn't your keeper you know!'

I just shot him a look and bounded up the stairs two at a time as he made his way to the kitchen. I stopped at my great-aunt's door, barely waiting for her response to my knock before sticking my head round the door.

'Hello, Great-Aunt! No, I can't come in — I have to dash. I just came to say I am out for the day. I'll come and see you when I get back!'

'Oh!' There was no missing the disappointment in her voice. 'With Tim?'

I shook my head. 'Nigel,' I told her.

'Oh!' This time there was more than

disappointment in the monosyllable. But I wasn't sure whether it was disapproval or concern I heard until she added, feelingly, 'Take care!'

A sense of freedom, almost a lightness of spirit, took hold of me as we left the Hall behind us. I could not help wishing that it were Tim I was with, but I soon settled down to enjoy the day and the outing and make the best of the company I had!

'Sophie told me that Hilda said someone had cut a tuft of fur off Marmalade,' I remarked, giving voice to what was still very much on my mind.

His reaction was remarkably similar to that of his mother. 'And how would she know?' He demanded. 'The damn cat was always losing fur and leaving great tufts all over the place. She is just imagining things!' He sounded impatient and the look he threw me was decidedly irritated. 'Look, let's forget the cat, talk about something else. Sure, I know it's upsetting for poor old Hilda, but enough is enough. I for one am sick of hearing about it and speculating who did it and why.' He shot me a sideways glance. 'Agreed? No more dismal dead cat talk?'

I nodded. Nigel could stop me talking about Marmalade but he couldn't stop me — or anyone else — wondering. I racked my brains to think of an acceptable subject for conversation. 'What sort of business are you involved in?' I asked, trying to sound genuinely interested. Nigel's face seemed to close up and he didn't answer for a moment. I hadn't come to terms yet with British reserve and the way they seemed to resent what we Aussies merely regarded as a friendly interest in the affairs of our friends and neighbours.

'Oh, this and that,' he replied vaguely. 'Property, investments, that sort of thing, you know.'

I didn't, but pursuing the query further didn't seem like a good idea. Anyway before I could reply he had turned the tables and was asking his own questions.

'What about you? Did you work or were you a student? I understand your mother had a business, some sort of a shop, did you help in that?'

The way he dismissed my mother's antique business as 'some sort of a shop' needled me, along with the fact that he, it seemed, could question me all he liked while skating over my own queries. It seemed we were not starting our day on a very harmonious note.

8

I decided that, good or bad start to the day, I was going to make the most of this unexpected outing and enjoy myself. I must admit that once we were on the open road Nigel turned out to be a pleasant companion. He pointed interesting landmarks out to me as we travelled and filled me in on the city we were approaching.

'Birmingham is our second biggest city,' he told me, 'overlapping into Warwickshire as well as Staffordshire.' We were by now well into the suburbs though to my eyes accustomed to vast stretches between cities, it seemed to me that we had been in continuous suburbia since leaving Stafford.

'I have an appointment this morning and another this afternoon,' Nigel told me. 'But I can meet you for lunch, say at 12.45?'

'I can look after myself,' I told him, 'if you are busy.'

He smiled. 'I should have phrased that differently. 'I should like to meet you for lunch' would have sounded better!'

'It would,' I agreed. 'If you really would like to meet me, then I would like to meet you.'

By the time we parted and he had given me explicit instructions where to meet him and how to get there, I was beginning to think that maybe I had judged him too harshly after all. He was really being very nice, very nice indeed, today. I spent the intervening time doing nothing more intellectual than wandering round the shops. Particularly the big department stores. I had few people back home to take gifts to so was not preoccupied by searching for suitable items amongst the touristy gizmos. I did, however, buy a wad of postcards to send to friends. This was the first real chance I had to think of holiday shopping. On my day in Stafford with Tim I had, to be truthful not given much thought to anything but him. On my way back to my rendezvous with Nigel I passed a large travel agency and decided to spend some time in there after lunch planning where I would go when I left Elwood Hall. For at that point in time I had no doubt that I would move on — and fairly soon.

Lunching à deux with Nigel proved to be a more pleasurable experience than I had expected. He was not only an entertaining host but as he turned out to be the sort of man always able to attract the attention of waiters, the excellent meal he treated me to in the luxurious surroundings of what I, personally, described as a 'plush' restaurant, was both relaxing and boosting to morale! The bottle of wine he insisted on ordering with the meal no doubt helped me to see him in a pleasant rosy glow. Certainly by the time I tottered forth into the outside world I had quite revised my early unfavourable impression of my cousin, who was not, I reminded myself, actually my cousin at all. A point he had managed to bring up over lunch.

When I reached the warm haven of the travel agent's office I was more than glad to sink into an inviting armchair with an armful of brochures depicting the high spots and particular charms of just about every bit of the British Isles. I refrained at this juncture from getting details of continental holiday destinations. Scotland particularly appealed to me with its pictures of brawny kilted men tossing the caber (whatever that was) or playing the bagpipes against a background of purple mountains.

I got up and went over to the nearest desk to get more details. What I got were brochures of what seemed to me terribly expensive all inclusive tours. I explained that was not what I really had in mind.

'Couldn't I camp, or something?' I suggested tentatively.

'You would be a bit cold at this time of the

year! But yes, if you wait a month or two no doubt you could.' I felt the eyes of the sophisticated and glamorous girl behind the desk, rake me from head to toe and back again. 'Or you could probably stay in youth hostels,' she informed me.

I thanked her and agreed that I probably could. I could also, I thought, stick with my original intention when I left Australia, of working my way around the British Isles. I would keep the glossy brochures anyway; they might help me decide where to aim for next if nothing else.

By the time I met Nigel at the car park at the appointed time I was well fired up in my enthusiasm to continue my travels and quite buoyed up by the thought that I had at least given myself the impetus to leave Elwood Hall. A determination that was given a boost when I returned to my room a while later. I slapped the brochures down on the bedside table planning to study them in peace before presenting myself downstairs at the dinner table. I pulled off my boots, wrapped my scarf tighter round my neck and burrowed under the quilt after switching on the small heater. Central heating, I thought, would be nice. As I leaned over to pick up my travel literature I noticed a white envelope with my name on it propped up against the bedside lamp. It had not, I was sure, been there this morning when I had dressed to go out with Nigel; though I had been in such a hurry I could easily have missed it.

I turned it over in my hand, slid my thumb under the sealed flap and tore it open. Inside I could see a small plastic bag — nothing else. I pulled it out and my breath caught in my throat. Inside was a large tuft of bright ginger fur — cat fur. For a moment I was too stunned to think straight, then the question hurtled through my mind. Who had put it there? Why? Was it a warning — or a threat? A cold shiver that had nothing to do with the icy climate in the room shook me and I slammed the small packet down on the bedside table as if it had scorched me. Sophie's words rang in my head: 'They cut a tuft of fur off him, isn't that odd?'

It was more than odd; it was downright sinister, especially as this very tuft of fur had been placed by my bed in a gesture — of what? Not friendliness, I was sure, and had probably been put there by whoever had been responsible for the cat's death. The person I still thought of, in my own mind, as the murderer.

Unable to rest any more I flung back the quilt and swung my feet to the ground. Of all the disturbing thoughts to enter my head at that moment the most disquieting of them all was that someone was coming to my room while I was out — or asleep. First the appearance of the key and now this much more sinister gift. I felt an uneasy ripple of fear run down my spine. I knew I had to get away — I could not endure to stay in this house. Making such a decision and acting on it were, however, poles apart. I longed for someone to confide in and as Tim's dependable and kind features swam into my inner vision I decided to try once again to contact him. Hard on the heels of that thought came the one that he might have tried to contact me while I had been out today. I pushed my feet into a pair of shoes, dropped the scarf on the bed and hurried downstairs to see if there had been any calls for me during the day. I almost collided with Harry Ingram crossing the hall on his way back to the kitchen.

'No.' He shook his head in reply to my anxious query. 'Hilda may have taken a call though, or . . . ' He seemed loathe to mention who else might have been the recipient of a call intended for me.

Hilda had the same reply as her husband. 'No, I took no calls for you,' she assured me. 'But — well that doesn't mean there wasn't one — someone else could have answered the phone. If they did it should be on the message pad by the phone in the hall, did you look?'

'No, I didn't think.' Actually I hadn't even realized there was such a thing. 'I'll go and have a look now.' As I turned to leave the kitchen she added. 'If your grandfather answered the phone — on the extension in his study — there probably won't be a message there.'

I hurried back into the hall, there were a couple of brief messages but neither was for me. I stood hesitant and irresolute. The mere thought of facing my formidable and antagonistic grandfather in his 'den' made my heart jump into my throat. Instead, I picked up the receiver and dialled Tim's number. Again it was answered by the pleasant female voice I had heard before. I guessed it must be the aunt he had told me about. She sounded genuinely concerned when she explained that he'd had to go out again. 'But he did ring you. In fact he called you twice and left a message each time for you to ring back as soon as you got in. He said he had given a number where you can contact him this evening.' She sounded kind and concerned. I wished I had accepted Tim's invitation to go there when I arrived instead of determinedly heading for my own relatives!

I put the receiver down slowly into its cradle and my glance fell again on the message pad. There was definitely nothing for me. I was about to turn away when I noticed indentations on the paper and that the previous sheet had been torn off roughly as if in a hurry. Some inner prompting made me pick up the pad and tilt it to the light. Examining it closely I could distinguish my own name and 'Tim', followed by a number. This, alas, was much harder to read as the other messages had been written over it. Why on earth hadn't I asked his aunt if she had the number where I could reach him?

I replaced the pad with a sigh and turned to find Nigel standing at the foot of the stairs watching me. To my fury I felt myself flushing guiltily as if I had been caught with my fingers in the till instead of endeavouring to read a message that had been intended for me anyway. Our eyes met for an instant, then he smiled and came towards me.

'What's the problem, Maggie?'

There seemed no reason not to tell him, after all whoever had made sure I didn't get any word from Tim and who had sought to scare me with the cat fur, it couldn't have been Nigel for he had been away from the house all day.

'There was a phone message for me,' I told

him 'But someone has removed it, and I believe there was another one that hasn't been given to me either!'

'Is that all? Heavens, by the look on your face I thought a really major disaster had hit you!'

'But that's not all!' I protested, and even while some inner voice prompted me to keep quiet about the packet of fur, I went on. 'I found Marmalade's fur — the tuft that Sophie said had been cut off him — by my bed.'

Now he laughed outright. 'Now you are getting carried away. I told you the damn cat left bits of fur all over the house!'

'Did he put them in little plastic bags and envelopes first?' I demanded.

'What? Oh, come on Maggie, you are letting this get to you!'

'Come upstairs then and I will show you!'

He followed me back up the stairs and I rushed over to the bedside table where I had left the wretched envelope. It wasn't there. I searched frantically, on the bed, under the bed, on the dressing table — even in the drawers. There was absolutely no sign of it. Finally I was forced to admit defeat. 'It was there,' I insisted.

Nigel shrugged. 'I believe you — thousands wouldn't!' he quipped facetiously. 'Come on.'

He held out his hand to me as the gong for dinner echoed up from the hall below. 'Come and eat!'

I had little choice but to accompany him. But I did not take the proffered hand. I was inwardly seething, first over my lost message, secondly because of what I felt was his patronizing attitude and last, but by no means least, with myself for failing to find the damn envelope.

I walked out of the door ahead of him and marched firmly down the landing towards Great-Aunt Sybil's door intending to see if she needed help getting down the stairs. There was no reply to my knock, only a raucous screech from Ozzie. Still burning with righteous indignation I marched down the stairs one step ahead of Nigel only to pause near the bottom at the sound of raised and angry voices coming from the direction of my grandfather's study. It was not so much the voices that caught my attention but what they were saying, for it seemed that I was the subject of the dispute. A door must have been opened for at that moment I heard my grandfather's voice say clearly, 'No, Sybil, Maggie must not be told — ever. I forbid it!'

I froze, straining my ears to hear more, hoping to find out what it was I must never be told, but all I could hear was an answering rumble, presumably my grandfather, before the elderly brother and sister appeared. My grandfather was driving his wheelchair with a little less abandon than usual to allow Sybil, leaning heavily on her cane, to keep alongside him. I pretended not to notice them and with my head held high hurried into the dining-room ahead of them. I waited till the whole family had taken their seats before looking round the table and asking with an air, I hoped, of complete innocence, 'Did anyone take a telephone message for me while I was out today?'

There was a moment of complete silence before my grandfather looked down the table and met my gaze calmly. 'I did,' he said. 'I would have told you before but it did not appear to be important.'

'Who was it?' I asked, looking him squarely in the face.

'Someone called Tim, said he'd ring again. That was all,' he told me meeting my gaze unblinkingly.

I looked round the table; everyone seemed preoccupied, no one, it seemed, was going to admit to taking the message that had been torn from the pad.

We seemed such a normal family gathered round the dinner table that I wondered for an instant if, after all, I had imagined that envelope of cat fur and its brief appearance in my bedroom and was perhaps just being a bit fraught about my message, or non-message, from Tim. After all, what possible motive could anyone have for deliberately keeping it from me? So I reasoned, but deep down I was scared and something told me I had cause to be.

I let the conversation ebb and flow, only joining in when a remark was addressed to me directly. For the most part I concentrated on doing justice to Hilda's excellent cooking. Yet every time I raised my eyes it seemed that my grandfather was looking in my direction. He did not seem particularly anxious for me to see him observing me however and when we might have made eye contact he always looked away. Somehow I found this unnerving and the fact that it was rattling me also made me angry.

The meal over, everyone seemed to go his or her own way — the two girls to watch a video in their own room, Sophie, Natalie and Gerald to watch a current affairs programme on the TV. My grandfather wheeled himself off to his own room and Great-Aunt Sybil, Nigel and I found ourselves still sipping coffee amid the remnants of the meal. There was an uncomfortable silence; I guessed we were all wishing at least one other person out of the way, broken simultaneously by my great-aunt voicing the same thought as me. I was volunteering to help her up the stairs to her room when she said, 'Can you spare the time to help me upstairs, Maggie?' She glanced obliquely at Nigel as she spoke and I felt she would have said more if he had not been there.

'Of course!' I told her.

'Shall you come back down?' Nigel asked.

I didn't know whether my imagination was at work again or whether I really did see my great-aunt shake her head, very slightly, as if giving me a message.

'No, I don't think so,' I told him. 'It's been a long day. Enjoyable though,' I added hastily. 'But I think I shall pack.'

'Pack?' they exclaimed in perfect unison.

'Yes,' I said calmly, avoiding looking directly at either. 'I am moving on tomorrow. I — I've been here long enough. I should really have contacted you before landing on you!' I gave a nervous little laugh that sounded very hollow to my own ears and I am sure to theirs.

'But this is your home. We are your family — you are welcome here!' Great-Aunt Sybil at least sounded sincere.

Nigel scraped his chair back from the table. 'In that case I will say goodnight and hope that if you haven't changed your mind by breakfast time at least you will come back again soon, cuz!' I thought he was leaving the room but instead he walked round to where I was sitting, placed his hands on my shoulders and leaned down to kiss me lightly, but directly, on the lips. I felt myself blushing, whether at the total unexpectedness of it or because I was conscious of Sybil watching, her expression quite unfathomable.

'I have a busy day tomorrow, and may, or may not, see you before you leave. *If you leave!*' He turned on his heel and abruptly left the room.

I drained my already empty coffee cup to hide my embarrassment and felt the grounds gritting my throat.

'If you are ready, my dear?' Great-Aunt Sybil pushed herself up from her chair and groped for her cane. Harry Ingram came in to clear the table and I hurried to help the old lady as she struggled to her feet.

We mastered the stairs with greater ease than the night before. 'I am getting stronger,' Sybil declared. 'I guess the old adage 'use it, or lose it' applies to the use of one's legs as much as anything! I have been a very foolish old woman,' she added, more it seemed, to herself than to me.

When we reached her room she walked

across to her chair in the bay window. I noticed that the carved box that contained her tarot cards was lying on the small table in front of the chair. 'I am not ready for bed yet,' she told me. 'If you meant what you said and really intend to leave us tomorrow then I will excuse you. Otherwise I should very much like you to stay for a while and keep an old woman company.' As she spoke she drew the box forward and removing the cards unrolled their silk wrap and began to shuffle them; the expression on her face a most curious blend of concentration and unawareness. Perhaps because I felt no pressure was being put on me in any way to stay I did just that.

'Tell me about your day,' she said in a remote sing-song voice. I wondered why she was bothering to ask me, for her whole attention seemed to be on the cards and the sound of their soft but rhythmic rustle as they moved from one hand to the other like a coloured waterfall was almost hypnotic.

'We went to Birmingham, had lunch, it was interesting.' As I fumbled for words to describe my day she began laying the cards down in a pattern like a cross, I remembered seeing my mother do this — the Celtic Cross. I think she had called it. I found myself watching the cards fall into place with as much attention as if I placed as much

137

credence in them as my aunt did. When she had finished laying them out she sat silent for some time. Respect for her, if not for the cards, kept me from breaking the curious spell that seemed to enfold her.

'I do not think you will be leaving us just yet' she told me without looking up.

'Oh, but I am!' I declared. 'I intend to go first thing in the morning. I have a job to go to,' I lied. Suddenly getting away from this house seemed a matter almost of survival and I was not going to be told otherwise by a deck of cards.

She stabbed at one of the cards with her forefinger. I looked at the figure of a woman bound and blindfold. 'You will not go because you cannot,' she told me. 'Look — you cannot see the way to get out of the situation you have put yourself in.'

I shivered in spite of the fact that the room was warmed to the point of fugginess by the electric blow fire she always seemed to have going full blast. I wanted to ask her the meaning of some of the other cards she had laid out in the spread. Particularly the significance of the death card and one of a knight in shining armour astride a white horse and carrying what appeared to be a full goblet. I wished now that my mother had been able to keep her promise to teach me how to read the cards or that I had taken sufficient interest in the past to learn something of them for myself; but her mood suddenly changed and with one swift movement she swept the spread up and returned them to the deck before wrapping them in their scarf and consigning them to their box.

She turned to me brightly. 'Now, tell me why you think you must go?'

'It's just, well, I can't stay here for ever. I need to earn some money and I do want to see something of Britain before I go back.'

'You are planning on going back to Australia, then?'

'But of course! I came really for a sort of extended working holiday. After Mum died I felt the need to get away — a complete change of scene,' I told her. She nodded; I felt she understood and was encouraged to go on talking. 'I got some brochures today in a travel agent; not that I am thinking of taking any of their luxury tours, but I thought it would give me an idea where to head next.'

'And did it?'

'Well, I thought Scotland sounded good. Or Wales. I suppose I want to see somewhere as different to Australia as possible!' I admitted.

'What sort of job would you hope to get?'

I shrugged. 'I don't really mind. I suppose the ideal would be one with accommodation,' I told her, though truth to tell that idea had only just struck me.

'Looking after children? Would you like that?' She sounded doubtful.

'I don't really know,' I told her truthfully. 'I suppose it would depend a great deal on the children.'

'And on the parents!' Great-Aunt Sybil's voice was tart. 'Why don't you take a look at some advertisements in papers and magazines and see what there is; or go to a good agency?'

I conceded that this was a good idea, dismissing the fleeting thought that it was strange that she, who a moment before, had predicted I would not leave here should be making such helpful suggestions. With uncanny insight she answered my unspoken question.

'I was telling you before what the cards were saying, not what I thought,' she said with a smile. 'Now — what about this boyfriend of yours? Have you managed to contact him yet?'

I shook my head.

'Then I suggest you do immediately.' She pointed to the drawer across the room in her bedside cupboard. 'My mobile phone is in there. Use that,' she commanded.

I got up somewhat dazed and collected the phone. 'Great-Aunt Sybil; I do believe you really are a witch!' I told her.

'But of course! Now, when you get him tell him you will be on the train that gets into Euston Station at 11.33 tomorrow morning. When you have done that you can phone and order a taxi to take you to the station; I'll get you the number while you are talking.'

To my joy and infinite relief I got through to Tim immediately this time. He promised to meet me at Euston and insisted that this time I would go back with him to his aunt's flat. I did not demur. I felt infinitely more secure than I had for days as I was swept along on this comfortable tide of protective organization. My great-aunt had one last admonition after I had finally settled her comfortably in bed.

'Don't talk about leaving or tell anyone you have ordered a taxi in the morning — not anyone,' she insisted. 'Just go!'

I promised I would do that, though secretly I knew I would have to tell Hilda at least. I was just leaving Sybil for the night having covered up the raucous Ozzie and done various other little chores for her and was on my way, when there was a tap on the door.

'That will be Hilda or Harry with my nightcap,' she said. But when I opened the door, it was neither of the Ingrams who brought her usual hot drink of Ovaltine, but, to my surprise, one of the twins.

'Hilda asked me to bring your drink up, Great-Aunt,' Jackie (or Josie) said. 'And she put one on for you, too, Maggie.' As I took the tray she pointed to one of the steaming mugs. 'That one is yours,' she told me.

I thanked her and bade her goodnight thinking that maybe I had been too harsh in my judgement of the two girls, considering them both sullen and unhelpful. I put the tray down on my aunt's bedside table and picked up my mug. I took a sip but it was far too hot to drink straight off. 'Would you mind if I took this to my own room? I should really get my things packed,' I asked.

'Not at all!' She smiled. 'It was thoughtful of Hilda to send up a mug for you.'

Back in my room I set the steaming drink down on the glass tray on my dressing table, locked the door carefully behind me and, crossing to the vast oak wardrobe, pulled my rather limited number of garments off their hangers and began stuffing them in my cases. I was filled with a pleasurable anticipation. By this time tomorrow I would be in London — with Tim. In that curious way cases have they were much more difficult to close than they had been when I came here, yet I had not added any new items. By the time I had pushed, pulled and sat on them I was ready for the hot drink that had by now been cooling for so long that it was no longer hot.

Ugh, I thought, it tastes a tad bitter. I had always considered Ovaltine rather on the sweet side. I drained it however before putting the mug down on the dressing table and making my way along to the bathroom to wash and do my teeth. I suddenly felt too tired to bath or shower. I would get up that much earlier I decided. Walking back along the landing I had a curious sensation for a moment, almost as if the floor were rising to meet me. However, it was only momentary, and once in my room I felt better. I locked the door and as an added precaution I pulled the chair across again and wedged it under the knob.

My God, but I was tired. My eyes would scarcely stay open. They did, however, long enough to register that a white envelope that was either the self-same one that contained Marmalade's fur or its double, was lying on top of the pillow. I picked it up, fully intending to open it and check, but such an overwhelming lassitude came over me that I could only flop down on the bed. I retained my senses long enough to kick off my shoes and pull the quilt over my body before I gave in to sleep, the envelope clutched in my hand.

9

I woke with a tongue that seemed to fill my mouth, a head that felt as if two demonic little men were hammering on the inside of my skull and the clear sun of a frosty winter morning streaming through my window (from which the curtains were drawn back) and bouncing painfully on my eyes. I hastily shut them again. But the sound of a chair scraping back echoed like thunder and made me re-open them. I turned my head slowly in the direction of the sound. An expanse of dazzling white made me close my lids again, but only in a long blink. Slowly I opened them and let my eyes travel upwards over what, I now saw, was Hilda's gleaming white apron, to her face swimming up there above me.

'You're awake.' She seemed to be informing me of the fact rather than asking. 'I've brought you some tea.'

I attempted to pull myself up to a sitting position, only to set those little men in my head going with their hammers. 'Ooh!' I groaned, putting a hand to my head and sliding down again on the pillows.

'Come on, I'll help you.' Hilda was firm. With her hands under my armpits she pulled me up to a sitting position, plumped the pillows up behind me and turning to the tray on the bedside table poured me a cup of tea. When she placed it in my hand it rattled audibly in the saucer.

'What is this?' she asked with a smile, and only as she pointed to the envelope still between my fingers did I remember finding it when I returned to my bedroom the previous evening. With a huge effort of will I attempted to gather my wits. I sipped the tea slowly. It did seem to have a reviving effect. At any rate the banging inside my head subsided to a monotonous thrum. I tried to tighten my grip on the envelope, which was difficult as I was also holding a cup and saucer.

'Oh, I don't know — probably just a scrap of paper.'

Unfortunately my dismissive air was so convincing that instead of deflecting Hilda's interest it caused her to draw the paper from between my fingers and open the unsealed envelope. She probably thought that she was doing me a service by confirming that it was of no importance, merely a scrap of useless paper. My brain was not yet working well enough to deal with the situation and I watched in a sort of fascinated horror as she drew out the inner, clear plastic envelope, and stared at the tuft of bright orange fur it contained. After what seemed an eternity she raised her eyes to my face; the expression in them was bleak — and accusing.

'Where did you get this from?' The words were hissed in a voice that was little more than a whisper.

I shook my head and winced at the pain. 'I don't know. It was here, by the bed, when I came back from the bathroom last night.' My voice sounded flat and unconvincing, even to myself.

She looked at me for a long minute. 'I see!' She said, and slipped the envelope in the pocket of her apron before turning away.

'Hilda.' I willed her to turn round, I wanted to yell at her; *No, you don't understand.* But she didn't turn round and all I could do was murmur helplessly to her back. 'It's the truth! I know nothing about it — it just appeared!'

The door clicked behind her and I realized I was talking to myself. In that moment of rejection I felt more utterly alone than at any time since my mother's death. Slowly I sipped the hot tea, drawing, in spite of myself, some comfort from it. Resolutely I fought back the tears that pricked behind my lids and swallowed over the lump in my throat.

As my tongue returned to a more normal size and the tattoo in my temples subsided a little I took stock of things. There was plenty to think about. First, how had anyone, Hilda or someone else, got into my room? Surely I was not mistaken in thinking I had locked the door and placed the chair against it when I came to bed?

I twisted my wrist to look at my watch. The cup sitting on the saucer in my other hand seemed to jump of its own volition as I shot up in bed. I just saved it from hurtling to the floor. The time was 11.30. I had not only missed my train but in exactly three minutes time Tim was expecting me to step off it at Euston. I gulped down the hot tea, adding a burnt tongue to the rest of my woes, flung the bedclothes back and, swinging my legs sideways, slid to the floor, groping for my slippers as I did so. As I snatched up my dressing gown I was conscious of an urgent need to empty my bladder. It was a call that over-rode everything else and had to be obeyed before I could begin to think straight.

As I hurried down the landing to the bathroom my senses cleared and by the time I returned to my room, though my head still ached with a dull thrum, at least I was beginning to think. My first instinct was to fly to the telephone and call Tim. Common sense told me that would be quite pointless for if he had kept his word, which I had no reason to doubt, he would be pacing the platform at Euston by now scanning the passengers disembarking from the 11.33 train.

I was brushing my hair rather gingerly because my scalp felt tight and prickly, when I paused to stare at my own somewhat wan face in horror as my slow brain came up with the unpalatable truth that someone — for some reason of their own — had deliberately kept me here. Why? And why again? I asked myself. What was the primary reason; was it to keep me at Elwood Hall or to stop me seeing Tim? Whichever it was, the means employed seemed a bit extreme for by now I had no doubt that the Ovaltine I had innocently, and gratefully, received last night must have been spiked. Thank God I hadn't managed to drink the whole thing.

'Look on the bright side,' I told myself. 'You are still here, not like poor Marmalade.' My attempt to cheer myself up sadly misfired for remembering the cat's very dead body and the terrible grimace on his face I felt more than a tingle of fear run up my spine. Who could I trust? Who was my friend? Recalling the look on Hilda's face when she saw the tuft of fur, Marmalade's fur, that I had been clutching so damningly in my hand, I did not feel I could expect sympathy and support from her.

As I sat there before the mirror looking at my own pale face the image of the tarot card, the one with the woman bound and blindfold, came to my mind. I felt exactly the same. My thoughts flew from this to Great-Aunt Sybil — surely there was someone I could trust? Yet even with the thought doubt came too. How did I know that she wasn't something to do with that doped Ovaltine? I tried to be rational and remember how she had been so helpful to me last night contacting Tim and arranging my 'escape'. But hard on the heels of that thought came the one that she was the only person who knew of my plans — therefore logically — she was also the only one who could stop me; for why, if no one else knew should they bother? It had slipped my mind for the moment that Nigel also knew.

I glanced again at my watch. I had been sitting here for nearly twenty minutes agonizing. By now Tim would have discovered I was not on the train. With any luck he would soon be back home. I had to phone him.

Having decided on some course of action I

felt marginally better. I left my room and headed downstairs for the phone. I wished it were in a less public place than the entrance hall.

When I picked up the receiver I discovered my head was still fuzzy enough to cause difficulty remembering Tim's number. I was sure he must have a mobile, but if he had given me the number I had forgotten it. On the first attempt I dialled the wrong one. When I finally got it right it seemed a long time before the receiver was picked up at the other end. I could feel my heart bumping against my ribs. But it was not Tim who answered.

'I'm afraid he hasn't got back from the station yet — he went to meet a friend,' his aunt told me. 'Can I give him a message?'

'Oh!' My voice seemed to stick in my throat and come out as a squeak. 'Actually this is the friend he went to meet.' I was gabbling now. 'Something, er, I — I was held up — I, er, missed the train.' Some instinct, intuition, gut feeling, call it what you like, stopped me from saying more. 'Tell him I am terribly sorry.' I paused and in the silence was sure I could hear breathing. 'Ask him to call me when he comes in, can you?' I deliberately waited before replacing the receiver and in the pause heard a distinct click. My feeling

151

had been right. Someone was listening in on an extension somewhere in the house. Slowly I turned round from the phone to make my way back upstairs. I had to trust someone and the only person seemed to be my great-aunt. As I moved away from the phone Natalie materialized from out of the shadows somewhere.

'Ah, Maggie — I hear you were not feeling too good this morning; are you better?'

'Thanks, yes.' I thought to myself that this was about the most pleasant Natalie had ever been to me as she asked me if I would be well enough to join the family for lunch.

'Or would you,' she asked, 'prefer a tray in your room?'

It would, I thought, be nice not to have to meet the rest of the family over the lunch table, but on the other hand I had great misgivings about a tray specially prepared for me after last night's experience.

'No, no,' I assured her. 'I'm fine now, really. I guess it was just a tummy bug — short and sharp!'

'Well, if you are sure.' She sounded doubtful and added sotto voce, 'You still look a bit peaky to me.'

I seemed to have two little voices inside me arguing with each other. While one was telling me how nice Natalie was being the other was remarking cynically that maybe what I took to be concern on my behalf was just wishful thinking, that she hoped I was actually feeling as peaky as she told me I looked!

When I eventually joined the other women of the household for lunch it was with one firm resolve; from now on I would be sure to only eat or drink the same as everyone else. Hard on that resolve came the reminder that I had not been the only person to have Ovaltine last night yet as far as I knew Great-Aunt Sybil was unharmed.

As far as I knew. I hadn't actually seen her this morning and as usual she was having her lunch up in her room. I resolved to seek her out immediately after the meal. A resolution I was not able to keep for we had only just seated ourselves when my grand-father wheeled himself in and took his place at the head of the table. He also took every-one by surprise and managed to place a dampener on what was already a very desultory conver-sation.

There were, in fact, only four of us spread round the vast table. I wondered why Hilda hadn't set the places all together at one end. Sophie and Natalie kept up some sort of a spasmodic conversation between themselves, my grandfather ate without speaking except for requests for something to be passed. I remained silent, my normally healthy appetite seemed to have deserted me and I ate little. Each time I looked up from my plate it was to find my grandfather's eyes on me with a look I couldn't quite fathom. When my eyes met his he would change his focus so that we never really made eye contact and I could guess nothing of his thoughts. I found this curiously unsettling. For once I wished the girls with their chatter were here, but they were at school.

I had risen from the table and was making my way to the door with the intention of going upstairs to visit my aunt when I was stopped by the gruff authoritarian voice of my grandfather.

'Maggie — I'd like a word!' It was a command not a request.

I followed him meekly out of the room as he wheeled himself briskly through the doorway. As I walked behind his chair through the hall and towards the door that led to the corresponding passage to the one leading to the kitchen I could not help but feel a tremor of curiosity both about what he wanted with me and about his sanctum.

I followed him down the flagged passage to a large room at the end, which again corresponded with the kitchen on the other side of the house. I looked round with interest, it was solidly and heavily furnished, a totally masculine room, the curtains were a heavy dark green chenille fabric and the walls, which didn't look as if they had been papered since Queen Victoria's reign, were almost completely covered by hunting prints and photos of horses with the odd picture of a dog for light relief. There were also a few gory hunting trophies similar to those in the main entrance hall. In fact the room was like an extension of the hall.

He wheeled himself behind a large oak desk and nodded curtly at a straight high-backed chair. 'Sit down,' he barked.

I sat, obediently, feeling just as I had as a child when summoned to the head's office for some misdemeanour in school. With my hands folded demurely in my lap I waited for him to speak. He seemed to have difficulty coming to the point. Totally ignorant of what he wanted to say to me I was unable to help him out so I sat and waited. I remembered overhearing Great-Aunt Sybil saying, 'She should be told', and wondered if that, whatever it might be, was what I was about to hear. It seemed not, for when he eventually spoke it was to ask me about my mother.

'Your mother, Maggie. Tell me about her.'

In my surprise at being asked to talk instead of listen, I knew I had to have been gaping rather stupidly. 'What about her?' I asked. I just stopped myself adding 'Sir' on the end of the sentence. As a result I knew I sounded abrupt, almost rude. He didn't seem to notice. Or if he did then he didn't mind.

'Anything and everything!' His piercing and rather cold, blue eyes bored into mine so that it took a real effort of will not to drop my lids before them. 'Most important of all — was she really happy?'

How can one answer that for anyone, even one's nearest and dearest? Perhaps even less easily for someone who had been as close to me as my mother. I didn't answer immediately but let my mind range back over the years.

'Yes, I think so,' I finally answered.

My grandfather sighed; whether from frustration at the brevity of my answer or some other reason I do not know. 'Did she — did she ever talk about her home here? Did she mention me?' His voice dropped on the last word. I guessed it took a lot of pride-swallowing to actually say those words.

My first impulse was to answer yes to both questions. But meeting those keen eyes again I knew that the least I could do was give him a truthful answer, no matter what it cost. I shook my head slowly. 'No,' I admitted. 'She never talked about you and very little about her home. Only snatches here and there.' I let my thoughts range back, grabbing at wisps of memory. 'She talked about the dogs, or rather one particular dog, a Labrador, she . . . ' I hesitated but he leaned forward and urged me on.

'Go on!'

'She always said that what hurt more than anything else was leaving her dog behind,' I said.

'That sounds like Angela.' His smile was thin. 'Tell me about her life in Australia — did she have a horse?'

I shook my head. 'No — she let me go to the local riding school when I begged for lessons, but I didn't even know she could ride herself,' I admitted.

He shook his head and said, more it seemed to himself than to me, 'How could Angie live without horses?' Then looking directly at me again he added, 'I always used to tease her and say she was brought up on mare's milk, she had so much rapport with horses.'

I listened in amazement. This was certainly a side to my mother I had never known about.

'What about this shop she had? Sybil tells me you told her she had an antiques shop. Was it a success? Did she make any money out of it? And your father — what about him?'

Sensing covert criticism of my dead mother in these questions, which seemed to be jerked out of him in a series of staccato barks, I jutted my chin and looked him straight in the eye as I replied. 'My mother built up her antiques business from very small beginnings to one of the best known in Melbourne,' I told him. 'As for 'making money', well she kept us both and educated me on it.'

'And your father?'

'I don't know anything about my father. I don't remember him. He left her when I was a baby. As far as I know she never saw him again and he never contributed anything to my upkeep or supported my mother.'

He crashed his fist down so suddenly on the desk in front of him that I jumped. 'Why didn't she let me know? Come home — bring you — or if she was too stubborn to do that at least ask me for money?'

'My mother was proud,' I told him. 'I don't know the full circumstances of her leaving home, only the little she chose to tell me when she was dying. Maybe you know the answer to your own questions better than I do. After all, you must know the reason why she left home in the first place. You were there — I wasn't!'

I saw a dull flush stain his cheeks. His fist clenched again and I braced myself for another crash on the desktop. Instead he slowly unclenched it and the vestige of a wintry smile touched his lips. For a moment we looked each other straight in the eye before he conceded. 'Damn it! I think I might like you after all. You seem to have more of your mother in you than your father.'

'It was my mother who raised me,' I pointed out. 'So, though I may have inherited things from my father her influence was paramount.' I was rather surprised to hear myself sparring verbally with this intimidating old man and wished I had been able to do it without sounding quite so, well, pompous. We sat in silence for a minute or two, each taking the measure of the other. Quite suddenly I knew that I liked him — and what is more I wanted him to like me. My lips quivered in a tentative half-smile which was rewarded with a similar quiver in return.

When he next spoke the tone of his voice was almost warm; and certainly he sounded regretful as he slowly shook his head. 'She should have come home and brought you with her,' he said. 'I had no idea, no idea at all she was left on her own.' He shook his head again before adding, again more it seemed to himself than to me, 'What a waste — all those

159

years wasted, lost, because of her stupid pride!'

'You could have contacted her,' I told him. 'The pride, which I agree was stupid, seems to have been on both sides!'

'I had no address,' he excused himself. 'She knew where to find me.'

'No doubt you could have found out where she was if you had wanted to enough.' I did not intend to let him off the hook so easily. I was sure that my mother would have come home, or at least written, had she known of his accident.

For a few minutes he sat, lost to me in his own memories. Then he looked up and smiled and such was his charm that I found myself smiling back. 'Pride causes a lot of grief,' he asserted. 'I will now swallow mine to apologize to you from the bottom of my heart for treating you as I did when you arrived.' He held his hand out to me across the desk. 'Will you shake hands with a stupid old man and say, 'Pax'?' he asked.

I leaned forward and placed my own hand in his, feeling his fingers close on mine in a vice-like grip.

'Pax, Grandfather.'

For a moment as we looked into each other's faces there was both understanding and affinity between us and I felt that, given a chance, I could love him dearly.

'We must talk again,' he said as he loosened his grip. 'There is so much more I want to hear and there are things I must tell you too.'

I rose to my feet, sensing that, for the moment, this was a dismissal. When I reached the door I turned back for a moment and offered a tentative smile. He looked suddenly so forlorn as he watched me go that I was tempted to cross the room to him, fling my arms round him in a hug and tell him how glad I was to have found a grandfather.

How bitterly I wished afterwards that I had followed that impulse.

10

I left my grandfather fully intending to visit my great-aunt next, but once again I was thwarted in my good intentions. As I closed the door of the old man's study behind me I was accosted by Harry Ingram, in fact when I turned round in the passage I almost bumped into him. He must, I thought, have been waiting for me to come out. I moved away from the door thinking he wanted to go in but it seemed it was me he was waiting for.

'Could I have a word, Miss Maggie?' he asked deprecatingly. My egalitarian Australian upbringing made me wince inwardly, once again, at the 'Miss'. Why for heaven's sake couldn't he just call me Maggie?

'Of course.' I told him, and waited for him to say whatever it was he had to say but he looked round him anxiously as if the dim passage were filled with lurking eavesdroppers.

'Perhaps you wouldn't mind coming to the kitchen?' he asked.

'Not at all,' I assured him. Wondering what he needed to talk to me about that couldn't be said where we were. I followed him through the entrance hall and down the other flagged passageway, almost identical to the one we had just left, and into the kitchen.

Hilda was standing behind the table, her fingertips resting lightly on its surface. She didn't appear to be actually doing anything and I guessed from her attitude and the way she looked at her husband as we came in that she was waiting for me. Mr Ingram closed the door firmly behind him but stayed near it giving me the sensation of being trapped between them. The idea that I had been brought here to be interrogated put me on the defensive so that I was totally unprepared for Hilda's apology.

'I want to say I am sorry . . . ' she began, her fingers now tapping a light tattoo on the tabletop. 'I — I misjudged you, Miss Maggie. I thought you had something to do with Marmalade's death. I think now I was wrong, so I would like to say I am sorry.'

Though the words were convincing enough there was something about the flat tone they were delivered in that left me feeling she didn't entirely mean what she was saying. Before I could reply however she burst out with a fresh accusation, and this time she knew what she was saying.

'But it was that fur — that tuft of fur! Can you explain what it was doing in your hand?'

A sudden lassitude born of despair overtook me. I pulled out a chair and sat down at the table, half turning to Mr Ingram as I did so. 'Please, can't we all sit down and talk this through?' I begged. 'I can tell you that it is as disturbing for me as it is for you.' I wanted to add *if not more so* but sensitive to Hilda's feelings I felt she might take that as a belittling of her grief over the death of her much loved pet.

Slowly she pulled a chair out opposite me and sat down, and her husband, seeing that I didn't look as if I was going to make a bolt for it, joined us at the table.

'Please, Hilda.' I looked directly at her, willing her to believe me and stop looking at me with an expression as wintry as the outside world. 'Please,' I repeated. 'I want you to believe that I honestly do not know how that envelope with . . . with Marmalade's fur in it, came to be in my hand.' Then I told her how it had previously appeared and disappeared from my dressing table making me wonder if I was seeing things.

She listened intently and, it seemed to me, her expression softened very slightly and her stiff posture relaxed. I saw a significant glance pass between the two of them. I knew I had interpreted it correctly when Mr Ingram cleared his throat.

'I think we should tell her everything, Hilda. After all she does seem to be involved,' he said somewhat portentously.

'Yes, I think you should explain things a bit, if you can, because, as you say, I am involved — whether I like it or not, which I don't.' I was emphatic, but shocked to hear my own voice tremble on the words.

'We don't think that Marmalade was killed deliberately,' he said slowly. 'We think it was an accident — a mistake.'

I heaved a sigh of relief. 'Well, that's a good thing!' I exclaimed. 'It wasn't very nice thinking there was someone around who would deliberately kill a lovely animal like Marmalade.' I was aware that my relief was not shared by the Ingrams who were both looking at me sombrely. 'Isn't it?' I asked hesitantly, looking from one serious face to the other.

'You don't seem to understand,' Mr Ingram spoke slowly and with patient emphasis as if I really were very dumb. 'Marmalade was poisoned all right; but not deliberately, like most cats he was an inveterate thief, he paid for it with his life.'

'You mean ... ' I said slowly as comprehension dawned on me. 'He stole some food intended for someone else and it killed him?'

165

They nodded in unison. 'Yes — that is exactly what we mean,' Hilda said, her eyes fixed on my face.

'But who?' I demanded again. 'I mean, who would want to kill whom?'

'Who indeed?' Mr Ingram sounded enigmatic. 'We thought you might be able to come up with an answer.'

'Me?' I was aghast. 'Why should I? What would I know about anything?' I looked from one to the other, surely they didn't think I had anything to do with what now seemed much more serious than a case of cat poisoning but one of attempted murder.

'We don't know!' Hilda let out her breath in a long sigh.

I leaned across the table and looked into her face. 'Hilda, please, believe me. I had nothing to do with any of this and I don't know anything about it. And by the way, I've been a victim too, I am pretty sure something was in that Ovaltine last night. Would I do that to myself?'

'You might!' Hilda sounded implacable. 'If it had been tampered with, then it only knocked you out for a bit; it wasn't lethal. What better way to establish your own innocence?'

Suddenly it was all too much; I dropped my arms down on the table and as my head followed them I burst into noisy tears. Surprisingly it was Harry Ingram who rose and put his hand lightly on my shoulder for a second.

'Don't take on so. Hilda was only giving it to you straight; I'm sure she doesn't really think . . . ' He tailed off, probably doubting my ability to hear through my own loud sobs.

I looked up and across the table at Hilda, gulping down my tears as I did so. I searched her face anxiously and saw a slow smile take over. With immeasurable relief I gave another choking gulp, sniffed and managed a shaky smile.

'No,' She told me. 'I don't really think that; I was just trying to make you see how things could look.' She shook her head as if trying to clear her own confused thoughts. 'But, Maggie, if you didn't do it, who did, and who are they aiming at?'

'I don't know. I just don't know!' I turned to Harry Ingram in appeal. 'You know the people in this house much better than I do. Who would do this? And why, for Heavens sake?'

He was so slow answering that at first I wondered if he had heard me. 'There are undercurrents here,' he said at last. 'Nobody knows everything, we all know a bit of the picture. It's like a jigsaw, everyone has a few of the pieces and until we get them all together we can't finish the picture.' I appreciated his simile but found it anything but comforting.

'I wish I had never come!' I cried with feeling, 'and I wish I could get away. I should have left early this morning, but you know what happened.' I pushed myself up from the table. 'But I don't have to stay. I shall leave — now.' Then, as the thought struck me, 'has there been a phone call for me?'

Both Ingrams shook their heads. 'Not as far as I know,' Harry told me. With his words I felt my resolve to leave weaken slightly, but not entirely. If I couldn't go to Tim and his aunt well then I should just have to find somewhere else to stay in London. I was beginning to understand why my mother, having left, never attempted either to return or to have any communication with this household again.

I walked over to the door. 'Thank you,' I said as I turned back into the room, 'for believing in me. I expect I will see you to say goodbye but if I don't then I'll say it now. I am going up to say goodbye to my Great-Aunt Sybil before I go.' I opened the door and walked out, aware of both their eyes on my departing back. They don't believe me — they don't think I intend to go, I thought as I crossed the main hall on my way to the staircase and my great-aunt's room. I found her, to my surprise, dressed and in her chair when I opened her door.

'Ah, Maggie!' She smiled a welcome and indicated the chair opposite her. 'How did your little chat with Adrian go?'

I must have looked blank for she hastily clarified. 'Your grandfather, my dear. I understand he had you in his study for a little chat, isn't that so?'

'He did invite me in to his room, but he didn't really tell me anything, did you think he intended to?' I could not forget that scrap of overhead conversation between them.

'I just wondered what he wanted to talk to you about,' she said soothingly. I was sure she wanted to know more than a general idea, but she was looking deliberately vague and I knew I would get nothing more specific out of her at the moment. I wondered how she knew I had been talking to my grandfather, but she was obviously well informed about everything that went on in the house in spite of her isolation, for she had expressed no surprise that I was still here when I should have left early this morning and been safely in London by now.

'I have come to say goodbye.' I told her.

'You are determined to leave then?'

'Why — yes.' I looked at her in surprise. 'You seemed to think that would be best last night,' I reminded her.

'That was last night,' she retorted.

I looked at her in amazement; all my old doubts and worries about whom I could and could not trust in this household came flooding back. I was still gaping when there was a brisk knock. In response to my great-aunt's brisk 'Come in' the door opened and Nigel walked across the room towards us.

'Ah, Maggie. Up on your hind legs I see. Feeling better?' Before I could answer he had reached my great-aunt and leaning down gave her a light peck on the cheek. 'I'm glad we haven't lost her, aren't you?' he asked lightly.

'We might do yet. She tells me she is determined to leave. See if you can persuade her otherwise.'

I stood listening to this exchange feeling anything but happy, for one thing I heartily dislike being discussed in the third person as if I were not there, and for another I was, literally, struck dumb by my great-aunt's change of tack. Last night it seemed she could not get me away from the place fast enough albeit for my own wellbeing. Today she was doing her best to persuade me to stay.

'Well, I'm going!' I almost yelled. 'I just came to tell you.'

'Are you expecting us to chain you and throw you in the dungeon?' Nigel's voice was mocking. 'Come now little cousin, would we do that?'

To tell the truth I was not at all sure, no doubt they had a cellar if not an actual dungeon.

'To show my harmlessness and my goodwill towards you I will even help you leave,' Nigel assured me now. 'You only have to say the word when you are ready and I will chauffeur you myself to the station.'

In spite of my innate distrust this seemed too good an offer to resist. 'How about now?' I asked. 'My cases are packed, just about. I can be absolutely ready in ten minutes at the most!'

'Ten minutes it is,' Nigel assured me. I hurried to my room to fling into my bags the few remaining things and in exactly nine minutes was presenting myself to him in my great-aunt's room. I bent and kissed her while over my head she bade Nigel to take good care of me.

'I will, indeed!' he assured her. There was nothing in the tone of his voice that I could take exception to yet I was filled with unease as I left the room with him. Maybe it was because I was almost sure that when I turned round from kissing my great-aunt goodbye I had seen him winking at her.

I was so anxious to get away from that house that I did not bother to say goodbye to anyone else. I did, however, stop by the phone and scan the message pad as I hurried through the hall on our way out. There was nothing for me. Tim had not rung back. I swallowed my hurt and unease telling myself I would soon be with him in any case.

As the car sped down the driveway through what was, by now, the gathering dusk, I stole a sideways glance at Nigel. As if aware that I was looking at him he turned in that moment and smiled at me. In spite of myself I had to admit that he was good-looking and of all my relatives he had shown me more friendliness than anyone, with of course, the exception of my great-aunt. It was because my thoughts were running along these lines that I probably smiled back more warmly than I intended.

'You are a funny little thing,' he commented now, his attention on the road as we moved out into the traffic.

'What do you mean?' I bridled indignantly. It was not the way any girl wanted to be described by a personable young man.

'You get so het up — work yourself into such a state over minor matters,' he explained. This did nothing to soothe me.

'What's so minor about a cat being

murdered, me being doped and things mysteriously appearing and disappearing in my bedroom? Not to mention someone coming in when I am either asleep or not there?' I demanded indignantly.

'You see, there you go again; all het up! Now, suppose we are a bit more realistic. A cat died, not uncommon — cats do die, after all he was no chicken, or should I say kitten. You think you were doped. In reality you may have just had a germ passing through you; you probably haven't even fully recovered from jet lag yet, and anyway you've had to cope with a very drastic and sudden change of climate. As for things getting lost and found and people getting into your room, well, don't you think that could be put down to genuine forgetfulness and a rather too vivid imagination?'

'I didn't imagine the vet's report on Marmalade,' I reminded him.

He shrugged dismissively. 'Silly cat probably ate some slug bait in the garden or something.'

It was only when I was reliving this conversation in my mind much later that it occurred to me that there would be little reason to put slug bait down in a garden that was blanketed in snow and ice.

Nigel took his hand off the wheel for a

second and patted my knee. 'See what I mean, little cuz? Most of your problems are in your mind.'

He sounded so reasonable and so convincing that I almost believed him. The lengthening distance from Elwood helped. Suddenly I peered through the windscreen. Even though I had only done the journey between the Hall and the station once, in the opposite direction, I had noticed some of the landmarks and I was sure we were not heading for the railway station as we drove through the town.

'Where are you going?' I demanded. 'This isn't the way to the station!'

'You are quite correct, it isn't!'

'What are you doing? Where are you taking me?' Alarm sharpened my voice to a sort of shriek as all my old terrors rushed back into my mind.

'Calm down! I'm not kidnapping you, if that was what you are thinking.'

I did my best to think rationally, loathe to confess that I had been thinking precisely that.

'Here you are again making a big drama out of little events; you have just missed one train to London so I am taking you out to an early dinner before I see you safely on your way,' he told me, speaking in that soothing voice that in reality I found so irritating. 'And over dinner I shall do my best to persuade you that you are grossly overreacting and that such precipitant flight is neither necessary nor advisable!'

I wanted to tell him not to be so pompous, but I was hungry and the idea of a good dinner to while away the time rather than waiting at a dreary station was appealing. I was not, however, about to cave in easily. 'That you won't do!' I asserted. 'I intend to be on a train to London before nightfall!'

'We'll see,' he remarked complacently as he turned the car into the short driveway of what looked like another country mansion. The large sign at the gate however informed me that it was in fact a hotel and restaurant.

'I brought you here because they start dinners at six and, more importantly, the food is terrific!' As he locked the car doors he glanced at his watch. 'Five-forty, that means we have time for a drink.'

He shepherded me into the hotel lobby in a proprietorial manner, checked that a table would be available for us at 6 p.m. then led me to the bar for a drink. At first I tried to order a plain fruit juice; caution suggesting to me that it might be better to steer clear of alcohol till I had got the residue of last night's concoction well and truly out of my system.

'Have a sherry?' he suggested.

I was about to firmly decline when I saw the amusement in his eyes and blushed to remember how I had nearly choked over the sherry on that first evening. I looked him squarely in the face and said demurely, 'Thank you, that would be nice. But not too dry please.'

I found it only marginally more bearable than the very dry sherry so popular with the ladies at Elwood Hall but by sipping it slowly I managed to drink it without pulling too many wry faces. I tried to ignore the rather light-headed feeling it was engendering in me.

By the time we made our way to the dining-room I was feeling both hungry and happy and ready to do full justice to what turned out to be, as Nigel had promised, truly great food. I even let myself be persuaded to drink a glass of the wine he ordered with the meal. No one could fault Nigel as a dining companion, I found myself relaxing (probably due to the wine) and actually enjoying his company. He had the knack, when he chose, of making a person feel they were important — to him. After the events of the last twenty-four hours it was a heady feeling! It was only when he calmly ordered coffee for us both that I demurred.

'But Nigel, do we have time? What time does the last train to London leave?'

He glanced at his watch then smiled across the table at me. 'I think you've probably just missed it,' he said with ill concealed delight.

I looked at him aghast. 'I can't have. It's early yet, there must be more trains to London?' I protested.

He made a great pretence of thinking. 'I believe there is — in about an hour. So calm yourself and just relax!'

I managed this — on the outside at least — but inwardly I was seething. I had no intention either of being caught like this again. I drained my coffee cup and rose from the table saying as I did so, 'Thank you for a very nice meal, Nigel, now if you will excuse me I must ask the receptionist to call me a taxi to take me to the station.' I forced a saccharine sweet smile as I made my way firmly to the reception desk.

I was aware that Nigel was following me but he was not, it seemed, about to make a scene in these surroundings. As I reached the lobby a young man was just going out through the swing door; there was something familiar about that back view, as the revolving door took him into the night I caught a glimpse of his face. It was Tim!

11

As I entered the lobby it seemed to me that Tim, for I was sure it was he, had been getting directions from the receptionist. I appealed to her now. 'That man. Where was he going, can you tell me?'

She immediately bridled and replied stiffly, 'I don't think I am at liberty to divulge that, madam.' The last word was tagged on the end and somehow she made it sound like an insult.

Throwing caution to the wind I begged, 'Please tell me!'

She began to bluster again but Nigel who by now was standing just behind me, cut in. 'We are supposed to be meeting him,' he lied. 'So if you could just tell us where he is going to it would save us a deal of time and trouble.' He flashed her his most charming smile as he spoke and his voice was silky.

'Well, sir, I suppose it won't do any harm. He was asking the way out to Elwood.'

'Come on!' In my excitement I grabbed Nigel by the arm. 'We must go back — hurry!'

So, after all, I found myself heading back to

the Hall. A fact which Nigel had no intention of letting pass without a wry comment or two. I barely listened as my mind was preoccupied with a thought that had lodged itself there. Why should Tim ask the way to Elwood when he had been there before? Unless, and this was even worse, I had made a mistake and it was someone else. But no, I was sure it was Tim, and equally sure that he had not seen me.

When we arrived back at the Hall Tim's car was parked at the front door and he himself was on the doorstep having what appeared to be an altercation with Harry Ingram. I hurled myself out of the car and up the steps in time to hear the latter saying firmly, 'I am sorry, sir. Miss Maggie is not here. She has gone out to dinner with Mr Nigel.'

'Tim!' I almost tripped over my own feet as I reached the top of the steps and grabbed at his coat sleeve to save myself. As I did so I felt another arm, Nigel's, encircle me.

'Steady, darling!' he murmured, but in a voice quite audible to Tim as well as me. I endeavoured to silence him with a glare.

'Oh, Tim!' I spluttered. 'I was coming back to London, truly, in fact I am on my way — or was when I saw you just leaving the hotel, so — so I came back. What are you doing here anyway?' My words seemed to tumble out like so much confused garbage; there was so much I wanted to say, and ask, and none of it was coming out right. I saw the light in Tim's eyes fade as he looked from me to Nigel who still had his arm round me in an attitude of affectionate possession. I tried to shake myself free.

Once more Tim looked from me to my cousin. 'I was worried about you when you didn't turn up this morning, and when you didn't return my call.'

'I thought it was the other way round,' I said abruptly. '*You* didn't return *my* call.' I pulled myself free from Nigel's unwelcome embrace and turned angrily on Tim. Though I directed my anger outwards in reality most of it was directed at myself. What on earth had happened to the independent woman who had so recently left Australia to see the world?

'Look!' I could hear a shrill note in my voice. 'I'm getting tired of this. I rang you, Tim, to apologize for missing the train,' I couldn't resist adding, 'Due to circumstances quite beyond my control. I left a message for you to call back. As far as I am concerned you didn't, though you say you did. Now here you are chasing me up looking all hurt and aggrieved. As for you, Cousin Nigel, I don't belong to you or anyone else in this family . . . ' I subsided, my anger having dissipated as quickly as it had flared. All I had achieved was a stupid scene and nothing to resurrect the independent person I wanted to be.

Tim gave me a look of, well, I preferred not to analyse it, then turning on his heel started down the steps. One step down he froze in his tracks before spinning round again as a bloodcurdling shriek rang through the house followed by running footsteps and the sound of sobbing. We stood there, all of us, literally rooted to the spot, as the twins ran into view. One was holding a handkerchief to her mouth and the other was screaming hysterically. With one accord we moved into the hallway, Tim included, in fact it was he who grabbed the sobbing girl and gripped her arms firmly as he demanded. 'What is the matter? What has happened? Tell us!'

The screaming twin, the one whose arms he held, stopped screaming and began to hiccup; both girls stared at him with eyes wide with horror.

'Come on,' he said, more gently now. 'What is the matter? What has happened?'

The other twin, the one with the handkerchief held to her face, now slowly lowered it and in a voice scarcely above a whisper and her eyes fixed on his face muttered, 'Grandfather!'

The hiccupping twin nodded. 'It's Grandfather,' she reiterated. The single word galvanized Harry Ingram into action. With a speed quite astonishing in a man his age he was across the hall and heading down the right hand passage towards my grandfather's room. Nigel followed only marginally more soberly. Tim let the girl's arms drop to her sides and looked at me; I met his eyes for an instant then turned my attention to the twins, both were sobbing uncontrollably now. Instinctively, we all stayed where we were and waited for information. Feeling the cold air blowing in through the open door I closed it and moved further into the hall followed by the others.

Nigel was the first back. He looked at us with hollow eyes before turning to the phone. He said nothing, but his white face spoke volumes. We stood there, a small silent tableau, watching him dial. I was just close enough to him to see that his hand was shaking. I failed to catch the actual words he spoke but could not miss the agitation in his voice, for the twins were both sobbing now, not overly noisily but in a miserable snuffling way. Tim and I stood and waited for Nigel to finish on the phone. When he finally turned towards us he seemed almost bereft of speech. Finally he blurted out, 'He's dead! The old man is dead!'

'Oh!' My hand went involuntarily to my mouth so that I stood there in much the same attitude as Jackie, or Josie, had done a few moments before.

'What? A heart attack? A stroke?' Tim asked.

Nigel shook his head vehemently, as did both twins in unison.

'No!' The single syllable exploded into the silence. 'No — he was shot!'

'What do you mean — shot?' I could hear the edge of hysteria in my own voice. I pressed the back of my hand against my mouth and let my teeth bite into the flesh as I fought for self-control. The twins going to pieces was more than enough.

'I mean what I say. He was shot — or he shot himself — with his own gun!' Nigel, too, sounded fraught and shrill.

For the second time I felt a strong arm around me, only this time I didn't move out of its circle but drew comfort from it. For a moment we all seemed frozen, then Nigel moved towards us speaking to me, and Harry Ingram came from the back of the house, he moved a deal slower than he had before and it seemed to me that he had changed in a very short time from an old man to an extremely elderly one. I dragged my eyes from his face, now almost as grey as his hair, and gave my attention to my cousin.

'I am sorry, Maggie,' he was saying. 'But it looks as if you will miss the last train to London after all!'

'I'll take her with me!' I felt Tim's arm tighten slightly as he spoke.

But Nigel shook his head. 'I am afraid not. No one can go anywhere until the police have been.'

Harry Ingram seemed to have pulled himself together somewhat. 'I must tell Hilda — and inform Mrs Talbot and Mrs Smythe.' He gestured rather vaguely in the direction of the lounge. 'You had better all go and sit down by the fire.'

Obediently we all moved across the hall. My numbed mind was grappling with the problem of just who Mrs Talbot and Mrs Smythe were. I was dropping down on to the sofa, with Tim beside me, before I realized he was referring to Natalie and Sophie sitting on another sofa. 'Great-Aunt Sybil?' I murmured vaguely to the room in general as Mr Ingram imparted the news to the two women and the twins went rushing towards their mother.

'Ah, yes — I will ask Hilda to tell her,' Mr Ingram replied. He looked round the room. 'Would anyone like anything? Tea or coffee?'

'Something a damn sight stronger for me, thanks,' Nigel replied, moving towards the drinks cabinet. Then he glanced at the still pale and snuffling twins. 'But yes, I think a pot of tea would be a good idea.'

'Very good,' Harry Ingram murmured as he left the room. I marvelled at his self-control, for even in the short time I had been at the Hall I had realized that he was the very prototype of the devoted family retainer and that a good deal of that loyalty was reserved for my grandfather.

I laid my head on the back of the sofa and momentarily closed my eyes. I felt drained of all emotion and utterly exhausted. The one thought uppermost in my mind was regret that I hadn't made good my escape earlier in the day.

With the arrival of the tea I was forced to bring my attention back to the room. At first I shook my head when I was offered a cup of tea but Tim simply got up, poured me one and put it in my hand.

'Drink up!' he told me.

Obediently I took the cup from him. 'A cup of tea,' I murmured. 'Isn't that the remedy of the English for all disasters?'

'Probably,' he retorted drily 'And it's not a bad one either.' He glanced across the room to where Nigel was pouring himself what looked like a stiff whisky. 'However, not being English I think I too shall avail myself of something a little stronger.'

I wanted to tell him not to be so pompous but it seemed like too much trouble so I slowly sipped the hot tea, which was, I noted, also very sweet, and watched him cross the room and fall into what, from here, appeared to be easy conversation with Nigel. Given the circumstances I couldn't imagine what they were saying.

We sat there in the lounge rather like actors on a stage set. But unlike actors we had no handy script, so for the most part we sat in silence. Only the odd murmur of conversation between Natalie and Sophie punctuated by a sniff or a hiccup from one or other of the twins broke the silence. I drained my teacup, thankful for its soothing warmth and sweetness, and then walked across the room to replenish it.

'Anyone else?' I asked, holding the teapot up.

There were murmurs of assent from the two older women and for a moment I was busy, thankful to have something, however mundane, to do. As I put the teapot down there was the scrunch of wheels on the gravel drive. We all held our breath and looked at one another. The slamming of a car door was followed, not by a peal on the bell but by the sound of the front door closing and footsteps crossing the hall. Sophie jumped to her feet as Gerald came into the room. He glanced round quickly as if taking in both the company and the solemn mien of everyone but before he could speak he was surrounded by his women folk. Both twins burst into noisy sobs once more at the sight of him and even the normally cool Sophie betrayed her emotion with a very audible tremor in her voice.

'Gerald! Thank God you are back!'

He patted his wife and daughters in a soothing sort of way, rather as if they were highly strung horses, as his eye once more roved round the room resting for a second on Tim with a slight frown of puzzlement. 'Whatever is the matter? What has happened? What are you all doing in here?' His gaze moved across the room to rest on Nigel as if he thought he was the person most likely to give him an explanation.

'It's the old man. He's dead.'

As Nigel spoke the twins clung to their father gasping between sobs and, almost in unison, cried, 'It was awful, Dad, just awful! We found him — he . . . he's been shot!'

Gerald looked round the room as if for confirmation, which he found in our faces.

'Oh, my God!' he exclaimed, and almost pushing his wife and daughters out of the way he moved across the room to help himself, as Nigel and Tim had both done, to the whisky decanter. He took a drink, refilled his glass then turned to the room. 'Just what happened?' he asked, addressing us as a group rather than any one individual.

There was a pause while we looked from one to the other to see who would be spokesman. It was Nigel who eventually told him. 'It's like the girls said — he has been shot. Or has shot himself. His own gun was used so it looks rather as if . . . ' He tailed off as if unable to think any more about it.

'His own gun? What do you mean — a shotgun?' Gerald asked.

Nigel shook his head. 'No, a handgun.'

'Do you mean a revolver?' This was the first time Natalie had spoken directly to anyone since news of the tragedy broke. 'But did he have one? Surely — '

Whatever she was about to say was interrupted by the sound of another vehicle arriving. The sound of the doorbell followed the sound of a car door slamming. We all sat as if frozen, waiting I suppose for Harry Ingram to answer the summons. When nothing happened Sophie got up and went to the door herself. It seemed to me as if we were collectively holding our breath but instead of coming back into the room she went straight across the hall leading the way to my grandfather's study.

The rest of that night was a confused patchwork of people and events. The body was not removed until after the doctor had left and the police photographer had done his work. The gun was taken away for fingerprint analysis and the police officer in charge had a few pertinent questions to ask about that too. Why did my grandfather keep such a gun, and where did he keep it, and who in the household knew about it? It seemed no one did, although that was certainly not the impression the other members of the family had given earlier on when Nigel had told us that he was 'killed by his own gun'. It was past midnight by the time the police left, and then it was with the promise of an early morning return.

'I hope everyone will be here,' the officer added raking us all with what seemed to me an all-seeing eye. I felt myself wilting, but by this time I was so exhausted and racked by emotion that I would have wilted at anything.

I realized that Tim was following the police towards the door. I snatched at his coat sleeve. 'Are you going back to London?'

He shook his head. 'Not tonight; I had

already made a booking at The Old Rectory.' This was the hotel where Nigel and I had dined and where I had caught sight of Tim at the reception desk.

'You were planning to stay the night?'

'Yes. I — have business in Stafford.' He paused then added, almost reluctantly, 'I was worried about you, too.'

'You were?' In spite of everything I felt my heart lift and knew that the corners of my mouth were turning up ever so slightly as I met Tim's eyes. We held each other's gaze for a moment; I think we were both trying to read what the other was thinking. I dropped my own eyes first, afraid that he might see more than I was ready to reveal.

'Well, I had better say goodnight.' I mumbled.

'Yes. Goodnight, Maggie.' He paused then added, 'I'll see you in the morning!' Before he left the room he nodded a brief goodnight to the others. I stood still for a minute listening to the sound of his car starting up then with a slight sigh I, too, bade the family goodnight and made my way wearily up the staircase to my own room. I paused for a moment outside my great-aunt's door, my hand moved to the door knob, then remembering the lateness of the hour and unwilling to face up to any more emotional scenes I went on to my own bedroom. I do not know a time when I had felt so utterly bone-weary, and soul weary, as I did when I let myself into the room I'd hoped never to see again. As I sank down on the bed I recalled with a sickening jolt that my bags were still in Nigel's car. This was all I needed. I was still sitting there wondering whether to go in search of them or simply to do without for tonight when there was a knock on my door.

'Come in!' I called automatically before remembering that I had turned the key in the lock when I came in. Dragging myself to my feet I crossed the room and opened the door.

'Your bags — they were in my car.' Nigel stepped forward and before I could collect myself was in the room.

'Thank you, I had just realized that.'

He put my luggage down but made no move to leave. There was a flush on his cheeks now and I caught the fume of whisky on his breath. I wondered how much he had drunk. I moved pointedly to the door.

'Thank you for bringing my things up,' I repeated, then added, 'I'm just about whacked,' hoping he would get the message.

He moved across to the door but instead of going through it he caught hold of me and kicked it shut with his foot. 'Shocked, or shell shocked, would be more like it,' he said thickly. 'Maybe we should comfort each other!' He pulled me close and the blast of whisky was now so strong I felt in danger of being intoxicated myself. My weariness came to my rescue here, for I was quite incapable either of responding or resisting. He bent and kissed me, but not on my lips for I turned my head slightly at the crucial moment. My lack of response seemed to effectively douse his enthusiasm for he drew back with a murmured, and slightly slurred: 'Another time then. Goodnight for now.'

'Goodnight,' I said firmly, opening the door as I spoke. To my relief he left, raising his hand in a sort of half-hearted salute as I closed the door on him and swiftly turned the key in the lock.

This little episode seemed to have drained the last scrap of energy and will power I possessed. I flopped on the bed, kicked off my shoes, pulled the quilt over myself and mercifully, in spite of all that had happened, I slept.

12

The first thing I was aware of when I woke in the morning was the leaden feeling somewhere in my solar plexus. It was a feeling that told me the world, or at least my particular corner of it, was not a good place. Full recall of the events of the previous evening flooded my mind as my body registered the fact that I was lying between the blankets and the quilt fully clothed. Pulling myself up to a sitting position I ran my fingers through my hair and swung round so that my legs hung over the side of the bed. I looked at my watch. I had, I saw, been asleep for my full quota of eight hours. Well, my watch may have told me that but my body certainly didn't. On the contrary, it felt unwashed and unrested. Anything but refreshed. My head felt heavy and thick, so much so that I was actually having difficulty acknowledging the painful reality of the last twenty-four hours. I shook my head in an effort to clear it, only to turn the dull feeling into an insidious ache. I decided a bath was the first thing on the agenda.

There was a glass jar of bright pink salts on

the shelf at the end of the tub. Whether they were put there for the use of guests or belonged to someone in the house I don't know, but I threw in a generous handful and revelled in the sweet frangrance that rose with the steam. My clothes were soon in a pile on the floor and I was gingerly testing the temperature of the water with one big toe while the rest of me shivered in the arctic atmosphere of the huge bathroom.

I count myself very fortunate in my ability to extract the maximum enjoyment from the moment, irrespective of what has gone before or what may be coming. By the time I stepped out of the water after a long relaxing soak and wrapped a large bath towel around myself I felt ready to face the coming day and whatever challenge it might bring. Rubbing myself dry and vigorously towelling my short hair, which I had also shampooed in an attempt to clear my fuzzy head, I made a resolution that, come what may, I would get away from this house before nightfall. As for my family, well, the events of the last few days had made being an orphan seem very attractive.

Following through this good intention I dressed in jeans and a warm sweater and repacked my bags before hunger forced me to venture downstairs in search of breakfast. Somewhat to my surprise I found it all laid out in the dining-room just like any other day, but, even more to my surprise, and certainly not like any other day, Great-Aunt Sybil was presiding over the silver teapot at the head of the table. The whole family seemed to be gathered, in fact there was only one place left at the table which, with a muttered 'good morning everyone', I took.

My great-aunt poured a fresh cup and passed it down the table to me. My mouth opened to say I would prefer coffee, but one look at her stern expression and the solemn mien of everyone else at the table and I shut it again.

I helped myself to cornflakes and glanced round; everyone else it seemed had either finished or was simply not eating. Attempting to appear totally unfazed I took a large spoonful of breakfast cereal; my chewing sounded like thunder in my ears. Nevertheless, I went on doggedly munching and crunching; determined not to notice the silence that enveloped everyone like fog. The effect on my appetite was dampening. I refused toast and sipped my tea, still wishing it were coffee. Over the rim of the cup I covertly studied the others. The twins were not in school uniform and neither Nigel nor Gerald was dressed for business. It seemed to me that with the rest of the family here I would scarcely be missed. With this thought in mind I scrunched up my napkin, dropped it on the table and pushed my chair back.

'Maggie!' I was arrested by Great-Aunt Sybil's voice, clear and authoritative. I had never heard her speak in this way before. Automatically, I dropped back into my seat and waited for her to say more.

'The police left instructions last night that we should all be here this morning,' she said, looking slowly round the table so that she appeared to be speaking directly to each one of us in turn. 'I think it would be a good idea if we decided what we are going to say.' She turned to the twins. 'Would one of you girls mind ringing the bell? I think Harry and Hilda Ingram should be here too.'

I looked round the table. Only I seemed to be in any way surprised by this remark. The two girls had got up in unison and managed to collide with each other as they crossed the room to the old-fashioned bell at the side of the hearth.

'What is there to say, but the truth?' I blurted out.

'Of course, dear cousin.' I felt the familiar rap of irritation with Nigel when he called me that. 'I think what Sybil means is whose version of the truth are we going to adopt. Isn't that so, Great-Aunt?'

The old lady nodded. 'But I wouldn't have put it quite like that,' she commented. 'I just think that whatever is said, or not said, we should all agree on the same line.'

'But,' I persisted. 'What is there any of us can say? Least of all me — I wasn't even in the house at the time.' I wanted to add that I wouldn't even have been on the doorstep when my grandfather's body was discovered but for a series of unfortunate accidents delaying my departure during the day. I glanced across the table and met Nigel's intent gaze on my face. I felt he was sending me a message and hazarded a guess that he wanted the same put forward for himself.

'The same goes for Nigel,' I added. 'In fact,' I blundered on, 'Tim was actually more involved than us. He was here before us!'

'Well, I do not think the police will be needing him,' Great-Aunt Sybil informed me. 'But you and Nigel are family and as such it is important that you are here to help the police.'

'Well, I'm not staying!' My defiance was borne, I think, of desperation. Once more I scraped my chair back and rose to me feet. I looked at the grim faces around me and finally settled on Nigel as being the least forbidding. 'Could you take me to the station, please?'

197

'Maggie!' My great-aunt's voice was both stern and angry. 'I do not think you have understood me. Neither you nor anyone else is going anywhere until the police have been. Afterwards . . . ' Her voice tailed off and she turned to the door as the Ingrams came in. 'Ah, I would just like a word about — about last night,' she began but was interrupted by the peal of the front door bell. As Mr Ingram turned back towards the hall, presumably to answer it, she threw me a look of exasperation. It seemed we would not, after all, have a chance to decide on a united version of the previous evening's events.

It was not the police that Harry Ingram ushered into the room but Tim. For the third time I leaped up from the table, this time with such vigour that I almost knocked my chair to the floor. 'Tim!' It was a cry of joy and relief. 'Can you take me to the station?' I gabbled without even greeting him properly.

His answer was cut short by the door bell ringing yet again. We all froze like children playing a game of statues and it was into this unnatural silence that two police officers, a plain clothes detective and a uniformed constable, walked. The detective looked round.

'Glad to see you are all here — and you too, Mr — er?'

'Fenton,' Tim supplied automatically before

catching my eye and giving the smallest of shrugs.

I walked back to my chair and once more dropped back into it. Inexorably it seemed the net was closing around me. I began to wonder if I would ever manage to escape from this house and this family and be footloose and carefree again. Had I known the shocks still in store for me, I think I would just have made a run for it there and then. As it was I sat back more or less resigned to the fact that, for the moment at least, I had no alternative but to remain. Looking up I saw Nigel's eyes on my face. I could not read what he was thinking but seeing me looking at him he flashed me a brief smile. At the end of the table Great-Aunt Sybil was also looking at me. Her expression was unfathomable; I did not know whether she was sympathetic or simply annoyed that I had defied her.

The detective was talking to the twins, his voice was avuncular, almost soothing. 'Perhaps you girls would come and have a talk to me about last night. I understand it was you two who found your grandfather?'

They nodded, both it seemed bereft of speech for the moment, then slowly got up and followed the detective from the room.

'Tim?' I repeated my question. 'Will you

take me to the station?'

The detective heard me and turned back momentarily to the room. 'Not just yet,' he said flatly before Tim could respond. 'If you don't mind, I would like everyone to stay here for the moment.'

Of course it was what I had expected. I shrugged in resignation. The strain was palpable, there was less than no effort to appear a happy family party or even, more appropriately, a family drawn together by grief. Outside the sun was shining and the snow was thawing, only small grey patches remained. I turned impulsively to the young constable who remained in the room.

'May we go outside?' I asked. For a moment he looked nonplussed. 'I would like to go in the garden,' I told him. 'That is all. Unless . . . ' I turned now to Tim. 'Would you like to see the horses?' I asked in an aside. Taking his slight nod as a 'yes' I rattled on to the policeman, ' . . . unless we go to the stables as well, but that is all, truly. I promise we won't even try to leave!' I assured him.

'I just had to get out of that awful oppressive atmosphere!' I told Tim as we picked our way over slush-covered paths in the direction of the stables. I was quite surprised to find that Tim really did want to see the horses.

'I was raised on a farm,' he told me, 'And what's more, I was an enthusiastic pony-clubber in my young days. I should have brought my camera,' he went on. 'These horses all looking out of their stables and the remnants of snow would make a great picture. In fact I have one or two equine commissions to do for some of the horse magazines back home,' he told me looking longingly at the horses.

'Oh, I see,' I said feeling flat at the thought that he had agreed so readily to come outside with me not because he wanted to be with me but because he really did want to see the horses. 'You are obviously a man of many talents!' I commented lightly.

As we walked along the line of stables looking at the horses it was more than obvious that when it came to equine knowledge he had a far greater store than I had.

'You would be able to carry on an intelligent conversation with my horsy cous-ins,' I remarked drily.

He turned and grinned at me. 'And you can't?' he guessed.

I shook my head ruefully. 'But I do like horses and I can ride. It's just when it comes to topics like hunting that I am somewhat floored. Partly I suppose because I don't really agree with it.'

'It never seems quite sporting to me either. So many people, horses and dogs in pursuit of one little fox.'

'Hounds!' I couldn't resist correcting him.

He grinned once more. 'Hounds,' he agreed. 'Anyway, it's irrelevant now it has been banned.'

We were leaning against the door of the stable housing one of the girls' ponies and I was stroking its soft muzzle. 'My mother was a very good rider,' I said, more or less thinking aloud as I remembered what Great-Aunt Sybil had told me.

'Did she teach you?'

I shook my head. 'I didn't even know she could ride. She never told me; even when I begged for riding lessons and she sent me off to the local school to learn. Don't you think that's odd?'

He was silent for so long that I wondered if he had heard me. 'Well, yes, it does appear so,' he admitted. 'But I guess she must have had a good reason for it.'

I sighed. 'I guess so, too. But I can't help feeling, well, I suppose hurt would be the word, that she never told me. Never talked to me much about her life here at all. Then when she died she charged me with coming back and making contact with the family she had left all those years ago and never been in touch with since. If I had known what I was walking into I wouldn't have bothered. Even though,' I added gloomily, 'a person's dying wishes are supposed to be sort of sacred somehow.' I turned to look at him as I finished speaking and at the same moment he turned and smiled at me. Our eyes met for a second and, in spite of everything, I felt a shaft of pure joy shoot through my being. He touched my arm lightly and even through my thick woolly jumper and parka I swear I was zapped.

'Come on, show me the rest of the horses before we go back in.'

As we returned to the house we met the twins crossing the hall. In spite of the fact that they were both red-eyed and snivelly there was an aura of self-importance glowing round them. The detective stood in the doorway of the lounge. He indicated that we should follow him as he turned back into the room.

'Now . . . ' He looked from one to the other. 'I gather neither of you were actually here when the old man was found?' He turned to me as he spoke. 'Can you explain what you were both doing on the front doorstep at that time?'

'That's right — when I came to see Maggie

I met up with her on the doorstep.' Tim hastened to explain.

'I had been out to dinner,' I added.

'I was calling to visit Maggie.'

We spoke almost in perfect unison.

'You are old friends then?' the detective asked. I half nodded and half shook my head; I wasn't quite sure how to answer this but while I was hesitating Tim nodded.

'Yes,' he replied. Fortunately the detective didn't pursue this. 'Maggie is coming to stay with us, my aunt and myself, in London, I came to collect her,' he continued.

I remained silent, realizing that in one sentence Tim had neatly sidestepped the whole business of my missing the train earlier in the day so that I did not have to answer questions on that or try and explain my mystery illness. I decided to say as little as possible and let Tim do the talking. By now it was mid afternoon.

After a few more perfunctory questions (or so they seemed to me — to the policeman they were probably quite pertinent) about my relationship to the other occupants of the house, how long I had been staying here etc., he included us both in a slightly wintry smile.

'I don't see any real need for either of you to remain here any longer.' He turned to me again. 'As long as you leave a phone number where you can be reached, you may go and stay with your friends in London.'

I thanked him and was at the door when he added, 'You will, of course, be back here for the funeral?'

I nodded and mumbled something in the affirmative. Truth to tell this was the first time I had thought about a funeral and returning for any reason had certainly not been in my mind. All I wanted to do was get away.

Nigel was the next one called in for questioning. If the detective was working to any system it seemed he was interviewing us in order of age from the youngest up. As we passed Nigel in the hall I was thankful my baggage was not in his car, at least I didn't have to ask him to let me have them . . .

He ignored us. Such was my farewell for I was in such a hurry to get away that I did not seek out anyone else to say goodbye. We were halfway to London before I began to feel guilty about that.

'I should have said goodbye to my great-aunt at least!' I told Tim.

'Shall we turn back?' he asked, so seriously that I thought he meant it, especially as he eased back the speed of the car slightly as he spoke.

'No!' I almost shouted. 'I never want to go near the place again.'

'Well, I am afraid that may not be possible.' He was quite serious now. 'Like the good copper said, you may have to be at the funeral; he was, after all, your grandfather.'

'Yes,' I admitted. 'But he only acknowledged my existence just before he died.' I still couldn't quite absorb the idea that he might have been murdered.

We drove for some time in silence then Tim asked me, 'What really happened to make you miss the train, Maggie? I was mad — then worried — when you weren't on it this morning. When I heard you had been trying to ring me I cursed myself for not giving you my mobile number.'

'I wish you had, I wasn't too rapt myself when I realized I hadn't a snowflake's chance in hell of catching that train,' I told him ruefully. 'It seems bizarre but I am sure I was deliberately prevented from catching it.' I went on to tell him just what had happened to me. Once I started talking I kept going and told him how someone seemed to be getting into my room and how things appeared and disappeared. He listened attentively with no sceptical interruptions.

'No wonder you wanted to get away!' was all he said when I finished.

I nodded. 'Yes. You have been a true knight errant.' I spoke flippantly, unwilling to let him see how emotional I really felt about his timely rescue of me.

I had talked so much that I hadn't noticed either the time or the miles passing so I was quite surprised to see that we were now driving into London. I pushed my problems to the back of my mind, sat up in my seat and peered through the windscreen at the exciting vista of a great city at night as it unfolded before me. I was as thrilled as any kid. This was London, one of the great metropolises of the world and I, Maggie Townsend, was part of it all.

'My aunt actually lives out in Barnes,' Tim told me, just as if he knew I was about to ask that very question. 'A bit quieter than being right in the city, in fact it has quite a village atmosphere, but it is lovely. Especially in summer.'

'Thanks, that's good to know as I head for it in the dead of winter.'

'Oh, it's nice now too! Her flat overlooks the river. In fact the Oxford and Cambridge boat race goes past so she has a grandstand view.'

By now we were leaving the city behind us and heading out for the suburbs. The bright lights had given way to quieter residential streets and when he finally stopped the car and we stepped out onto the pavement I could hear, or at any rate imagined I could, the lapping of the river on the other side of the road beyond the range of the street lamps.

Tim dragged my cases out of the car and I followed him through a brilliant yellow door and up a short flight of stairs to another door, this time bright blue, which opened as we reached it.

Tim was promptly enveloped in a warm hug of welcome by the vibrant woman who had opened the door to us. She then moved aside to let us step past her into a cosy room bright with pictures, rugs, throws and lamps at strategic points. I felt immediately at home.

Tim's aunt was, to say the least, a surprise. She was the perfect complement to the room, or maybe I should say the room was a sort of extension of her. Both she and the room were warm, colourful and slightly untidy. She was also much younger than I had imagined. In fact she did not fit my idea of an aunt at all.

'This is my Aunt Penny.' I suddenly realized that Tim was doing the right thing and introducing us. 'And this, Penny, is Maggie!'

I smiled and held out my hand, remembering I was in England and murmured politely, 'How do you do, Miss — er — Mrs . . . ?'

'I thought you told me this girl was an

Aussie, Tim?' Her voice was unusually deep and had a sort of bubbly sound, as if laughter might break through at any moment. Turning towards me she took my outstretched hand in both hers in what I found a most comforting and heart-warming grip even though it only lasted for seconds. 'Bless you, child. I'm not a Miss, a Mrs or even a Ms; I'm just Penny — to you at any rate. Now, sit down in the warm, have a cup of that coffee you can smell percolating and put me in the picture.'

With a great sigh of pure relief I sank back against a pile of vivid cushions; for the first time since I had landed in this country I felt secure. A CD was playing soft ambient music in the background, the gas fire popped and hissed companionably and the smell of coffee drifting out from the kitchen blended with a tangy aromatic scent from an incense stick just about to give up the ghost. In spite of the fact that this room was what I would call 'New Agey' and those I had grown up in with my mother had been 'Antiquey' there was an underlying similarity. Just as I recognized something in Penny that was akin to my mother although Mum never lost her habit of dressing like an English lady even after nearly a quarter of a century in Australia.

I leaned back in the chair feeling totally relaxed; the music, which I liked, but did not recognize, washed over me, the warmth enveloped me and the murmur of voices from the kitchen were infinitely soothing.

13

I did not realize I had dozed off until I heard the slight clatter of the tray being put down on an occasional table in front of me. My eyes flew open and I looked round in momentary confusion. The wonderful aroma of the coffee soon brought me to a full awareness of my surroundings however. I sniffed appreciatively. 'Ahh!'

Penny smiled at me as she passed me a steaming cup. 'It is a wonderful smell, isn't it? The smell of Heaven, I call it.'

'Yes, if the hereafter smells like this I shall be quite content.' I returned her smile. I liked this unusual woman who exuded such warmth.

In spite of the caffeine I felt my lids growing heavy again as I put down my empty cup. Penny immediately got to her feet and flashing me another of her warm smiles said, 'You look dead on your feet, or on your seat, a good nap is what you need. Tomorrow will be soon enough to start talking.'

I could only agree with her. Gratefully I pulled myself up out of the chair and followed her from the room with a brief goodnight to Tim. Too tired to do any more than give myself a 'lick and a promise' I crawled beneath the colourful duvet on the divan bed in the tiny spare bedroom cum box room that Penny led me into. So strong was my feeling of having come to rest in a safe haven that I was asleep as soon as my head hit the pillow. At least I guess I was, for the next thing I knew I was opening my eyes to a wintry sun peering through the chink in the curtains and the same wonderful fragrance of coffee assailing my nostrils. As I opened my eyes my hostess peered anxiously round the door. Seeing me awake she came into the room.

'Good, you're back in the land of the living.' She tossed a rich red velvet robe on to the bed as she spoke. 'I know you haven't unpacked anything so slip that on and come out to the kitchen and have some breakfast.'

Pulling the tie of the sumptuous garment snug round my waist I followed the coffee smell to the kitchen. It was larger than I expected and like everything else I had seen so far in this flat, colourful, cosy, and slightly untidy. I pulled out a cane stool and sat down at the breakfast bar in response to Penny's cheerful. 'Take a seat — coffee coming up.'

She drew up a stool opposite me and

placed the coffee pot between us, next to a breadbasket of warm rolls, a jar of honey and a butter dish. 'Help yourself!' She waved in the direction of the food.

As I spread butter on a hot roll and watched it melt I felt totally at home; something I had never felt at Elwood Hall. I smiled across the bench at Penny and as our eyes met I had the curious feeling that this delightful woman was going to mean something in my life.

'No wonder Tim likes staying with you,' I said impulsively, then looking round as if I might see him lurking in a corner, I asked, 'Where is he, by the way?'

'He had to go out, to see an editor he is doing some work for. He'll probably be back for lunch.' That was when I looked up at the clock on the wall and saw that it was nearly ten o'clock!

'Good heavens!' I exclaimed. 'I must have slept for hours!'

'About twelve, but I guess you needed it. You must be hungry now — so eat up.' She pushed the basket of rolls towards me.

I was more than willing to obey. 'Yes, I am hungry. I also feel deliciously decadent somehow breakfasting at such a late hour and wearing this wonderful garment.'

Penny flashed me her warm smile and

murmured something I didn't quite catch, but it didn't matter for I knew she understood perfectly how I felt.

'When you have finished I suggest you have a shower — the water is always hot — unpack, get dressed and generally make yourself at home. By the time you have done that Tim should be back and we can have lunch; here or out — just as you like. How does that sound?'

'Absolutely marvellous!' I asserted, draining my coffee cup and sliding down off the stool. 'But I shan't need to do much making myself at home; I already feel that — thanks to you.'

'Oh — get along with you and have that shower.' With a shooing gesture she sent me on my way.

The water was, as Penny had promised, hot; as I felt it cascade down on my face and bare shoulders I imagined all the horrors and general miseries of the last few days flowing away with the sweetly scented water (I had found a boronia scented shower gel on the shower caddy) as it gurgled down the waste pipe. With my usual ability to bounce back and see the bright side of things life was looking good again!

By the time I was scrubbed up, brushed up and dressed up, Tim was back and perched on one of the bar stools in the kitchen chatting to Penny. They broke off their conversation and turned in my direction.

'Feel better? You certainly look it.' Penny smiled.

Tim gave an inelegant wolf whistle which should have made me bristle with feminist indignation but only made me blush in feminine appreciation at what, I knew, was meant as a compliment.

'You look great and I've had a successful morning; the editor I went to see not only liked my stuff but also wanted more. Even better he paid me, so I'm treating you two gorgeous girls to lunch. I hope you're both hungry because I'm starving.'

It was a beautiful day outside, though the air had a crisp bite the sun was glinting on the Thames as it flowed past on the other side of the road. I could feel my natural joie de vivre rising and when Tim asked, 'Shall we take a bus into town or would you rather walk to somewhere local?' I replied without hesitation.

'Walk, please!'

So walk we did, and I could enjoy the almost village atmosphere of this particular part of London. In fact I found it hard to grasp that I was actually in one of the greatest cities of the world.

'Angelo's?' Penny raised a questioning eyebrow at Tim.

'Great. You do like Italian food, Maggie?'

'I love it.'

The beaming Italian, who I discovered actually was called Angelo, greeted Tim as a long lost relative. 'Thissa your girlfriend, yes?' He turned to me.

In spite of the embarrassment he caused me I could not help but beam back, so all embracing was the warmth he exuded. I shook my head.

'No matter! Soon will be!' Angelo declared, then seeing my confusion and Tim and Penny's amusement he added, 'Girlfriend for today anyway!'

It was a perfect day; I would hold it in my memory to return to whenever possible to look at and cherish in the days to come. I remember it as filled with sunshine, laughter, and good food and, most important of all, wonderful companionship. I wished it could go on for ever but of course, in the manner of all good things, it had to come to an end.

After a prolonged lunch punctuated by laughter Penny announced that she had work to do and regretfully would have to love us and leave us. Much as I liked her and enjoyed her company I have to admit that I did not mind being left alone with Tim and, from the way he smiled at me, I think he felt the same.

'Well, what would you like to do?' he asked as we got up from the table. 'What do you want to see? Or what have you seen?'

'Everything to the first question and nothing to the second,' I told him. 'All I have seen of London is the glimpse I had when I arrived off the plane with you.'

'Which is just about nothing.' Tim grinned. 'London is a pretty big place you know, so everything is a bit of a tall order, tell me something you are really desperate to see.'

'What I really want to see,' I told him without hesitation, 'are some of the famous landmarks, you know, Buckingham Palace, Trafalgar Square, Piccadilly Circus.'

'Then that is what you shall see,' he assured me. 'And the very best way to do it is on top of a double-decker bus.'

Either we were lucky, or it was Tim's magic, but we were able to secure the front seat on the top deck of each bus we scrambled on during our sightseeing tour. Tim turned out to be an excellent guide.

'Have you ever thought of doing this for a living?' I asked him. 'You seem to know the questions I am going to ask before I even ask them.'

'That's because I'm an Aussie too.' He smiled. 'All this was new to me once and

Penny took me round just as I'm taking you, and I guess I asked her all the questions you would ask — if I gave you a chance!'

I smiled at him, feeling warm and close to him, 'You're probably right,' I conceded. 'I had forgotten you were Australian.' Our gaze met and held for a second before I turned away to drink in the panorama of the great city unfolding before me through the wide front window. In that moment I had felt my heart skip a beat and the warmth I was conscious of seemed to be coming as much from inside me and from the right side of my body which was touching Tim, as from the warm interior of the bus. It was a good feeling, safe and secure. I was about to say I would be happy to stay here for ever when Tim shot to his feet, grabbing my hand as he did so.

'Come on, we get off here — we have an appointment with four lions and an admiral!' He threw the words over his shoulder as he headed for the stairs.

As we made for the centre of Trafalgar Square I gazed in awe at the four vast stone lions guarding each corner and then let my eyes travel up the tall column to the figure on top. It was just as I had seen it in pictures, even down to the crowds of tourists and pigeons; the only difference was I hadn't expected it all to be so big somehow.

'Gee!' I breathed as I gazed heavenward. 'It's awesome!'

I couldn't even explain quite what I felt standing here in this spot I had so often seen depicted in books and film. I felt somehow both insignificant and important all at once. I made an effort to put my feelings into words.

'I've always thought I was Australian, through and through,' I said. 'In spite of my English background. Yet standing here I feel a pride of belonging rather than the awe of a tourist.'

Tim gave my arm a squeeze. 'I agree, that's a bit how I always feel. Each time I come to England I make a point of coming here — a sort of pilgrimage I suppose to my roots.' He laughed suddenly and gestured to the huge column. 'Some totem pole, wouldn't you say?'

By the time we had made our way back to Barnes, by bus of course, a warm camaraderie had developed between Tim and myself. A feeling that on my part I knew could, with very little encouragement, develop into something much deeper. He, however, seemed to look upon me with the warm affection of a kindly elder brother rather than a potential lover. That being so I was determined to keep my own emotions in check.

I sighed as we stepped down from the bus

at the stop nearest to Penny's flat. 'Thank you, Tim. I really enjoyed myself.'

'Good!' Once more he gave my arm an affectionate squeeze. 'So did I, if it comes to that. And now I'm pretty hungry again so let's hope Penny hasn't been too busy to cook.'

Judging by the rich herby aroma that assailed us as we let ourselves into the flat, if Penny had been busy with other things she had also found time to cook up something appetizing for us.

'Hello, kids!' she greeted us. 'Perfectly timed — everything is ready to dish up. Come straight to the table, and you, Tim — open the bottle will you please?' She waved a wooden spoon in the direction of the small round dining table where a bottle of red wine stood with a corkscrew.

The meal, a rich pasta dish, garlic bread and red wine, followed by fruit and cheese, was delicious and I felt utterly and completely at home with these delightful people. I smiled broadly at them both, wanting to voice my thoughts but not quite sure what to say. How I wished I had accepted Tim's invitation and come here in the first place instead of heading off north to my own relations. Now I had met Penny and seen how very different she was in reality to the 'aunt' stereotype I had built in my mind, I knew she would have given me a warm welcome.

So lost was I in my thoughts that I visibly started when the phone shrilled in the background. Penny, who had jumped up to answer it, turned to me. 'It's for you, Maggie.'

'Me?' I repeated rather stupidly. I was about to add, even more stupidly, 'who can it be?' till I remembered that the only people who could possibly be calling me would be from Elwood Hall, and whatever it was they wanted I really didn't want to know. Nevertheless, I rose slowly to my feet with a sinking heart, and slowly crossed the room to Penny who was holding the receiver out to me.

'Hello?' My voice sounded flat, even to my own ears. 'Oh, hello, Nigel.' Involuntarily I glanced across the room towards Tim. His eyes were on my face and for a moment I thought I detected a concern that went far beyond idle curiosity but when my eyes met his he dropped his lids and concentrated on the apple he was peeling. 'Yes, sorry — I didn't catch what you said.' I realized Nigel had been talking but I hadn't taken in a word. With barely disguised impatience he began again; he was telling me about the arrangements for my grandfather's funeral the next day.

'I see. You mean I have to come back. Do I really need to come?'

'Yes, I think you do,' Nigel insisted. 'The police want everyone here and, well, as a member of the family you are expected to attend.'

'I suppose so,' I said reluctantly. Frankly I did not feel much, if any, sense of responsibility to the family I had so recently discovered.

'Great-Aunt Sybil is counting on you.' Nigel knew my weak spot and even though I suspected he was exploiting it I agreed to return.

'OK, I'll come.' My voice sounded grudging, even to my own ears.

'Good! I knew you would. I shall pick you up first thing in the morning.'

'I am sure I can get myself up there, no need for you to bother coming down for me.'

'It's no bother. I'm in London at the moment so I shall be there about 8.30 to pick you up. Just tell me the address would you? I only have the phone number.'

I put my hand over the receiver and turned to Penny. 'What's the address here?' I mouthed.

As she told me the address, I repeated it after her into the phone.

'I'll see you in the morning.'

'Bye,' I muttered dully into the mouthpiece but the dialling tone was already humming in my ear. Slowly I replaced the receiver into its cradle. 'That was Nigel. He's picking me up at 8.30 tomorrow morning. I have to go to my grandfather's funeral.' I spoke tonelessly and addressed my words to Penny but my eyes never left Tim's face. I saw the muscles tighten round his jaw line and when he looked up and turned towards me I could read nothing from his expression.

'I wish — oh, I wish I didn't have to go.' I crossed the room and slumped down in my seat at the table. Suddenly all the sparkle had gone out of the day and I felt incredibly tired.

'There was no need to say you would go with — him, with Nigel; I would have taken you, you know that.' Tim's voice was gruff. I knew he was angry with me and felt wounded by the injustice of it.

'No, I didn't know you would take me.' Even to my own ears my voice sounded cold and my eyes I felt were probably as hard as his when I looked up and met his gaze. 'I was expecting to go by train.'

Penny made a valiant effort to boost our flagging spirits and keep some sort of conversation going but when we had finished our meal and cleared away I made my excuses. 'I've an early start,' I apologized.

'And it looks like being a bit of a day.' With a rueful smile I bade them both goodnight and made my way to the little guest room. As I closed the door behind me I could hear the murmur of their voices but could not distinguish the words.

I packed my belongings before I climbed into bed where I lay awake, smarting from what I felt was Tim's unfair annoyance. The alternative avenue for my thoughts, the trip up with Nigel and the prospect of the funeral and meeting up with my family again did nothing to induce a restful sleep.

I was up early the next morning, but Tim was up even earlier. I found him in the kitchen making coffee and toast and pouring himself a glass of orange juice. He held up the jug with an inquiring arch to one eyebrow.

'Please.' I nodded. Then, unable to help myself I gave a deep sigh as I pulled out a stool and sat down at the bench. Tim poured me a glass of juice then hesitated before turning and taking out the two slices of toast that had just popped up rather noisily. He placed them in a small ceramic rack with extreme care before raising his eyes to my face.

'I owe you an apology.' His voice was stilted. 'Of course you have every right to travel with whom you like — it's just that . . . ' His voice tailed off. With a shrug he turned away as with another bang the toaster shot out more toast.

There was such a dejected droop to his back that I found myself muttering, none too graciously, 'Well, if you really want to know I would much rather be going with you. In fact I wish I didn't have to go at all — with anyone, in fact . . .' By now I was getting carried away. 'I wish I had never ever been near Elwood Hall in the first place.' To my horror I heard a crack in my voice and knew that if I didn't take a grip on myself I would soon be weeping salt tears of self-pity into my breakfast.

Tim turned round and faced me brandishing two pieces of slightly burned toast. He was almost smiling. 'You know what they say? 'Whatever relatives we draw, we smile and just excuse 'em!'' he quipped.

In spite of everything I smiled back, shakily. 'Well, I sometimes think mine take quite a bit of excusing,' I admitted, and went on to quote the remainder. 'But friends aren't given us by law — thank goodness we can choose 'em!'

Tim sat down opposite me, really smiling in the old friendly way. Then, suddenly serious he leaned slightly towards me. 'You do think of me as a friend, don't you,

Maggie? I hope so. I hope so very much — because I can assure you that's the way I think about you.'

His words should have warmed my heart. Instead they left an ache. I looked at his face, concentrating now on pouring coffee, and knew that I didn't want him as a friend; I wanted more — much more. I dropped my own eyes to my plate, as he looked up; afraid of what he might read there.

'Your — cousin . . . ' He hesitated slightly. 'Will be here shortly and I shan't have time to say what I want to.' In spite of myself my heart gave an absurd flutter.

'Which is?' I prompted gently through a mouthful of toast.

'That I want you to promise me that you will keep in touch — let me know it, well, if there is any trouble of any sort. I guess you need a friend as well as that family of yours.'

'I guess I do, and yes — I promise. But please — can I have your mobile number?'

He jumped up and went towards the phone, for a moment I wondered if I had annoyed him but he tore a scrap of paper off the pad by the phone and quickly scribbled on it. 'Don't lose it,' he admonished as he passed it to me across the bench. I smiled gratefully and mumbled my thanks as I shoved it quickly into my pocket.

The long silences between us were bad, but even worse were our brief and stilted attempts at conversation. I wasn't sure if I had unwittingly annoyed Tim or if he was simply preoccupied with his own thoughts. I pushed my plate away, excused myself and went to my room to put together my belongings.

Nigel was more than punctual; he was five minutes early. He arrived just as I was carrying my bags out of my room, which meant that I had no chance to make my farewells privately to Penny and Tim.

The former kissed me and assured me of a warm welcome when I returned to London. Tim did not kiss me but he did give my hand what I imagined, and hoped, was a meaningful squeeze. 'See you.' He sounded so Australian I was assailed with homesickness, or just dread of the day to come. I had a sudden gut wrenching memory of my mother's amusement when someone she was most unlikely to ever see again said it to her. Settling into the passenger seat next to Nigel I hoped with all my heart that Tim meant it.

14

Concentrating on getting away from London in the busy morning traffic Nigel was not inclined to make conversation. As for me, I felt leaden in every way, physically, mentally and emotionally. About the only feeling I was aware of was an illogical and most unfair anger with my grandfather for being dead and thus necessitating my presence at his funeral. I also felt a sense of betrayal that he was not there for me when I so suddenly and so desperately needed him. Equally unfair I know — but there it was.

Once we hit the motorway we picked up speed and Nigel relaxed sufficiently to make conversation. Without much success, for I found it hard to do much more than respond in monosyllables in spite of the questions whirling round in my head like so many fallen leaves in an autumn gale. The nearer we got to Elwood the tighter the knots in my stomach. Nigel's fast and rather reckless driving didn't help. I wished, oh, how I wished, that it were Tim driving me to what I was beginning to think of as a 'date with destiny'. Better still that I was still in London in the friendly atmosphere of the flat in Barnes. I told myself to stop worrying; I was on a simple mission to attend the funeral of my grandfather, that was all, and when it was over I would simply get on a train and return to London. And from there, I decided, I would get on a plane and return to Australia. Once back there I would do my best to forget that my English relatives existed. With the exception of Great-Aunt Sybil — although even she, I had to admit, was a trifle strange — they were an odd and not particularly lovable collection.

I was jolted back to the present moment by Nigel's hand placed momentarily over mine as it lay in my lap. 'Nearly there,' he told me, then giving my hand a slight squeeze before removing his own he added, 'Nearly home — your home.'

I looked at him sharply, what on earth did he mean? Elwood Hall was not, never had been and, as far as I could imagine, never would be, my home. Not in any sense that the word conveyed to me. His expression was inscrutable, so, as we were by now turning up the drive, I decided to ignore his remark.

At Elwood Hall the family were gathered in the drawing-room, waiting for the funeral cars to collect them. The atmosphere when I walked in was one that Mum would have described 'could be cut with a knife'. The hum of conversation, desultory as it appeared, stopped as I walked in and all eyes looked at me. The hostility was palpable, anxiously I sought my great-aunt and with relief saw that she, at least, seemed pleased to see me. I went straight over to her and kissed her wrinkled cheek. She caught my hand with her thin, claw-like one and holding it tight pulled me close so that only I could hear her urgent whisper. 'Oh, my dear — you shouldn't have come!'

Her words surprised me and I involuntarily drew back as if I had been rebuffed until I saw that the only expression in her eyes was one of loving concern.

'But I had to,' I protested, forgetting that so short a while back I had wished myself anywhere but en route for the funeral. 'After all, he was my grandfather.'

I was surprised at her first response, which was to shake her head as if in denial, but she changed it so quickly to a nod I thought I must have imagined it. 'Yes — yes, of course,' she said soothingly.

I was glad when we made a move to the village church for the funeral ceremony though I did not particularly care for the way Nigel had taken me under his wing. He was treating me with the sort of proprietary tenderness that suggested that I was the chief mourner and he was the chief comforter, by right. As both suppositions were so patently untrue I found his behaviour irksome, to say the least. I could not pretend to be a grieving granddaughter in view of the fact that my grandfather had barely acknowledged my existence and if I had ever imagined that I might like a closer relationship with Nigel my brief sojourn in London with Tim and his aunt, both of whom I was beginning to think of as 'real' people, had cured me.

The lovely old Norman church was full, it seemed half the village had turned out to say farewell to the old man. As unknown granddaughter suddenly returned from the Antipodes I was aware of their curiosity. I was also uncomfortably aware of Nigel's arm under my elbow steering me out behind the coffin on its way to the churchyard after the service.

Looking up from the open grave I saw the familiar figure of the detective who had interviewed each member of the household on the day of my grandfather's death. It was comforting to know that the law was keeping an eye on proceedings. Bringing my attention back to the family group round the open grave I met the eyes of my aunt, or step-aunt or whatever, Nigel's mother, Natalie. I found myself involuntarily taking a half step back as I felt the intensity of her gaze. At first I thought it was simple hate, then she smiled and I was confused. The more so as it was probably the first time she had ever smiled at me and this seemed an odd time and place to begin. I had the sudden uncomfortable sensation of being trapped and looked round to see if there was an escape route. Of course there was not. The open grave and the vicar solemnly intoning that gloomy bit about 'earth to earth, ashes to ashes' was in front of me and most of the village behind me. I tried to shake off Nigel's hand, which was still on my elbow but his grip only tightened in response to my rather feeble shrug. I reminded myself that as soon as this wretched business was over I was leaving this place — for good.

I was beginning to feel a bit like a dog on a lead as Nigel led me to the car to return to the Hall. 'There is no need to hold me,' I hissed. 'I can walk.' But he didn't release my arm until I was safely in the car and he was sitting by me. I turned away from him and looked out of the window just in time to see the tail end of a car disappearing from sight, it looked familiar, it reminded me of the car that Tim drove, for a wild moment I hoped that it was, but only for a moment for I had left Tim in London and he had certainly not mentioned coming up — and anyway why should he?

My mind was fully occupied as we drove back to the house with the knotty problem of how soon, or just how, I could make my escape. With each turn of the wheels I was feeling increasingly a prisoner. I felt guilty because again I was plotting to get away, if I could, without saying goodbye to my great-aunt or even Harry and Hilda, all of whom had been kind to me and done their best to make me welcome in a very strange, and at times, intimidating household. In spite of my turbulent thoughts I found myself walking into the gloomy and imposing hallway with the other members of the family. Nigel's hand still hovered close to my elbow. I did my best to appear calm and unfazed.

We made our way to the dining-room where someone, I have no doubt the Ingrams, had prepared a buffet meal of cold finger foods and a lavish array of drinks. I breathed in with relish the welcome smell of freshly brewed coffee. It brought me down to earth for I suddenly had the odd feeling that rather than taking part in this wake I was an outsider looking on. I was adamant in my refusal when Nigel tried to make me accept the sherry that was being handed round.

'Something stronger?' he asked, indicating the whisky decanter.

'No . . . ' I shuddered, I didn't like sherry but I detested whisky so it wasn't hard to refuse. 'Just coffee, please.'

He shrugged but fetched me a cup. As I sipped it I felt grateful for its warmth and relished the strong bitter taste. At least this should help me to keep my wits about me. I looked round the room for my great-aunt and when my eyes discovered her on the far side I was surprised to see that she was looking at me with a strange intensity, as I met her gaze she closed one eye in an unmistakable wink. Taking another gulp of the hot coffee and with my half-empty cup in my hand I began to thread my way through the crowd taking advantage of Nigel's attention momentarily on someone else.

I leaned towards Great-Aunt Sybil and kissed her lightly on the cheek as she took my hand and gave it a squeeze. I really liked the old lady; there was empathy between us that was totally lacking with any of my other relatives. I wondered briefly if I might possibly have found a similar feeling with my grandfather had we ever got to really know each other. Great-Aunt Sybil still held my hand so that unless I snatched it brusquely away I was forced to stay close. She spoke so softly she was almost whispering. 'You do realize don't you why they are all so interested in you?'

I shook my head. I had absolutely no idea. 'Well, I suppose because I am still the stranger?' I hazarded a guess.

Sybil shook her head. 'Quite the reverse, because they know you are the only true descendant of my brother.'

'But that is absurd . . . ' I glanced round the room, 'There is the whole family.'

'No. None of them are actually related to him by blood. Natalie is his stepdaughter, so her sons are not actually his grandsons. The same applies to Gerald's twin girls.'

'Oh.' I couldn't think of anything else to say as my mind grappled with this piece of information. Did they think — but surely not? I gaped at her implications of what the family might well be thinking. 'Was that what they thought I had come for? Is that why . . . ?'

'They were so hostile,' she supplied for me. 'But of course. That is what they would have done in your place, so naturally they assumed that you had come to claim your birthright from under their noses.'

'But I didn't!' I protested, and then as the unpleasant thought hit me. 'You surely don't think that?'

To my relief she shook her head so that her blue rinse curls danced. 'Of course I don't. As soon as I met you I could see exactly who you were and knew you were as true blue as your mother. Not for one moment did such a thought enter my head, any more than I would have thought it of my poor dear Angie.' I was pleased when she said this, but bridled when she referred to my mother as 'poor'. She was astute enough to notice this. 'No . . . ' she amended. 'It was not your mother who was poor, she moved on to another life. I was the poor one — left here without her and never hearing anything.' She paused and her eyes gazing somewhere into the past glazed with tears. 'Why didn't she answer my letters, do you know, Maggie?'

I stared at her. 'I can't tell you. I didn't even know she ever heard from anyone from here. If she did she never mentioned it.' I threw my mind back, trying to recall if Mum had ever said anything about letters from her old home or family. 'I do remember . . . ' I said slowly, frowning slightly with concentration 'her complaining about not hearing anything, she didn't actually say she had written but somehow she made it sound as if she had and no one had bothered to reply.'

Great-Aunt Sybil stared back. 'I see,' she murmured at last, in a voice so quiet I barely heard her. It was not the answer I expected, and was surprised that what I had told her seemed to please her, although I could not see why. I was about to ask her what she meant but a general movement among those present took my attention. I could see several non family mourners moving towards the entrance hall, heading for the front door while the immediate family seemed to be closing ranks. With a sinking heart I guessed that the dreaded moment when the family solicitor would gather us together to reveal the contents of my grandfather's will was imminent. I wished I could mingle with those who were leaving, but with my great-aunt clutching at my arm on one side and Nigel moving swiftly across the room to flank my other side I had little choice but to move with the family in the direction of my grand-father's study where the family solicitor, most appropriately called Herbert Wills, was already seated at the old man's desk shuffling papers in a business-like manner.

He peered over his spectacles at us as we all trooped in, gauging, I imagine, the various degrees of expectancy. 'Please — all be seated.' He nodded vaguely at the chairs dotted about the room, then cleared his throat, shook the papers in his hand, put them down on the desk and picked them up again. He looked round once more over his spectacles before pushing them back up to the bridge of his nose. At last he cleared his throat once more and began to read. I was so surprised at this display of nervousness from the one person I had thought to be totally in charge of the situation that I almost forgot my own concerns. Almost — but not quite.

I closed my eyes and almost my mind as he intoned all that dry legal stuff about this being the last will and testament of George Charles Henry Sinclair, made while within his right mind etc., etc., and only opened them a little when he started on what seemed a long list of bequests.

I felt glad for the Ingrams when I learned that they had been left the cottage they occupied in the grounds plus a lump sum and a reasonable annuity. I turned towards Nigel to express my pleasure but he was leaning forward, hands clasped on his knees, with such a look of concentration to which he now added a definite scowl, that I remained silent.

There were several more similar bequests, he had forgotten no one it seemed who had ever been of service to him in any way. By the time he had worked through to the twins, his step-granddaughters, I was very much aware of Nigel fidgeting at my side, his impatience and anxiety and, yes — his growing anger flowed from him in waves. I had become so absorbed in the drama playing out around me that I had almost forgotten that everyone seemed to expect me to play a key part in it.

He had left the girls several thousand pounds and their horses. Similar bequests had gone to other members of the family. I was so absorbed in working out exactly what the correct relationships between us all were that I barely heard Nigel's muttered comments though I could not help but feel the way he was fidgeting in his seat. I was so startled to hear my own name that I almost jumped up.

'To Margaret Elizabeth Townsend of 23 Hertz Street, Melbourne in the State of Victoria, Australia, the jewellery belonging to my first wife which is now in a locked jewel case in the safe in my study. The case has her mother's name on the lid as this would have been her inheritance had she outlived me. I also wish the said Margaret Elizabeth Townsend to choose any item out of the house that she would like as a memento of her visit, together with the sum of fifty thousand pounds to be given into the care of my sister Sybil and handed over at such time as the said Margaret Elizabeth Townsend leaves the country, or provides proof of her intention to do so.'

I was uncomfortably aware that the eyes of almost everyone in the room were turned my way, most with expressions of curious interest. The exceptions being my great-aunt, who was beaming approval at me and Nigel whose expression was that of a stunned mullet. His mother's look of shocked surprise turned to one of such sheer malevolent hatred as she stared at me that I felt myself shrink back into my chair with an involuntary shudder. I had no idea what I could possibly have done to deserve this and turned to Nigel hoping for some sort of explanation. He merely glared at me with an expression painfully similar to that of his mother and spitting out the single word 'Satisfied?' got up and walked across the room to his mother.

Feeling almost as if he had struck me physically I turned round to Sybil my eyes silently begging for an explanation. She merely gave my hand a reassuring squeeze and, murmuring 'I'll explain later' honed her attention in on the solicitor who had resumed his somewhat monotonous reading of what seemed an endless stream of bequests. I wondered how many of these could be paid out before the coffers were empty. A swift glance at Nigel's face and I guessed his thoughts were running along parallel lines with mine.

As I mentally reviewed my own inheritance I felt irritation rising in my throat, an irritation that was rapidly deepening to anger. What it really amounted to was the fact that I was being paid to leave the country. How dare my grandfather treat me like that, even posthumously? As I inwardly fumed and railed against him the thought blew into my mind that even in death he had refused to acknowledge me as his granddaughter.

I was jerked out of my reverie by the realization that the dry Mr Wills had finally finished reading the will and was shuffling papers together and mumbling something about 'hoping everything was clear to everyone'. As he spoke he looked round the room without looking at anyone in particular. A difficult task and one that made him appear rather furtive. As I watched him I realized with surprise that he was afraid of something — or someone.

There was a general murmur of assent from those beneficiaries like myself who hadn't really expected much, if anything, so were quite happy with what they got. There was an astonishing, and very loud, guffaw of laughter from Gerald. I looked at him in amazement for he was one of the few people who had not been mentioned at all in the will. I saw he was looking across the room at his wife and son whose reactions were anything but amused. Nigel was white faced and thin-lipped, his mother quite the reverse, so flushed and wild-eyed that I wondered for a moment if she were about to have some sort of a fit.

'I am glad you are able to see the humour of the situation, Father. Maybe it won't seem quite so funny when you are turned out and cannot find another soft billet.' Nigel turned back to the lawyer. 'Would you mind explaining once more exactly what I have been left?' His tone was clipped and cool to the point of being frosty.

Mr Wills ceremoniously cleared his throat and shook his papers, adjusted his glasses on his nose and after making a great show of finding the correct place began to read: 'To my step-grandson Nigel . . . '

'Yes, yes — I know my own name,' He interrupted rudely. 'Just tell me what I get — or don't get.'

Mr Wills cleared his throat and shook the will in his hand so that the paper rustled in protest. 'You get,' he said in a tone of ice, 'a part share in Elwood Hall, an equal share with the other beneficiary, your mother. All the contents, all goods and chattels, motor vehicles etc., become the property of Mr Sinclair's sister, Miss Sybil Sinclair together with a small house, currently rented out to an excellent tenant, in Stafford. There is a codicil,' Herbert Wills added with it seemed to me considerable satisfaction, 'to the effect that all those currently living in the house should continue to do so for as long as they wish.' He placed the document down on the table and added, 'You'll be aware of the, er, considerable mortgage on the property.' There was no mistaking his satisfaction now.

'I am.' Nigel got up and began to move towards the door. 'If this is some sort of joke it is in very poor taste. As the old man well knew keeping this white elephant of a place going without the wherewithal will be almost impossible.' He looked across at me, a look of pure hatred. 'I thought . . .' he began, but what he thought we were not destined to know for as he spoke his mother leaped to her feet and with an unearthly scream hurled an object and herself across the room in my direction. For a mad wild moment of hope I imagined I saw Tim before a blinding pain in my temple sent me slithering to the floor — and darkness.

15

I was only momentarily stunned, fortunately. The inkwell, which had been hurled across the room at me with such malevolent force, had only struck me a glancing blow but that was enough to make my temple throb and, putting up my hand to the pain it came away with blood on the tips of my fingers. What was so utterly terrifying was to open my eyes to look straight into Natalie's manically staring eyes. When I tried to escape their naked hatred I realized with heart-stopping terror that her hands were around my throat.

Through a swirling mist and choking pain I thought I heard her hiss vitriolic obscenities at me then realized with enormous relief that the pressure on my neck was easing and that strong male hands were prising her fingers away from my throat. Through the blur I thought I saw four hands. I must be seeing double, was my last coherent thought before the dark mist once more enveloped me.

I raised my head and endeavoured to open my eyes when I felt the cool rim of a glass against my lips and the warm smell of brandy in my nostrils. I sipped obediently and almost choked again as the fiery liquid hit my throat. Struggling to gain control of the situation, and myself, I pushed the hand holding the glass away and opened my eyes. I immediately shut them again; I had to be dreaming, what I was seeing could not be real. Slowly, I raised my eyelids. Unbelievably I was looking straight into a pair of familiar eyes, warm with concern for me. For a moment I really thought I must be dead.

'Tim — where have you come from?' I tried to say but my voice only came out as a sort of strangled croak.

'Don't try to talk.' That was Great-Aunt Sybil's voice just behind my head. I tried to turn to see her but my whole neck hurt and the movement set off the throbbing in my temple. I felt a hand on my shoulder, from the corner of my eye I could see the hand I had once likened to Ozzie's foot, now the parchment-like wrinkled skin and the long carefully varnished nails seemed quite beautiful and gave me enormous comfort. I wasn't at all sure quite what had happened but if I had Sybil behind me and Tim at my side I knew everything would be fine.

My somewhat woozy attention was caught by what appeared to be a scuffle at the doorway; I managed to focus all my attention in that direction and saw that the centre of the disturbance was my step-aunt Natalie. She was being removed from the room forcibly by a burly individual whose back view I was certain belonged to the young constable who had accompanied the detective when we had all been questioned after the sudden death of my grandfather. I saw the glint of metal and realized with a shock that what I was looking at were handcuffs. But I was even more shocked when I saw Nigel standing slightly to one side, watching this ignominious and forceful removal of his mother. His expression was one of glacial impassivity. I felt a cold shiver trickle down my spine as he watched her being led away, waited till he heard the slamming of car doors then turned his attention back into the room and specifically back to me. I think I must have given an involuntary shudder for I felt Sybil's fingers tighten on my shoulder in a silent message of comfort and support. Tim straightened up and faced him. Glancing swiftly up at him I was surprised, and somewhat reassured, to see his jaw tighten while at the same time the dark blue of his eyes seem to fade slightly and take on a glacial sheen. In silence we all watched as Nigel crossed the room towards us and waited tensely for him to speak.

He stopped just in front of me and gave a

small bow, his lips twisted in a cynical smile. 'Hard luck little cousin . . . ' His tone was even more sardonic than the expression on his face. I had no idea what he was getting at. I had not expected anything so though I was a little miffed at the wording of my grandfather's bequest I certainly wasn't feeling sorry for myself at all. 'No inheritance from Grandpa after all, and of course I can't afford to marry you now, but I am sure you understand, after all it would seem that we were both playing the same game. It was naughty of you to mess things up like you did; all the same Mother really shouldn't have gone off at you half-cocked like that.'

I was gaping at him feeling quite stupefied. What on earth did he mean? He may well have been hoping for a substantial bequest but such a thought had never crossed my mind. 'You have the house . . . ' I murmured, hoping somehow to placate him.

'The house?' The words burst from him in an explosion of fury. 'If you had the money, as you should have done if you had played your cards right, and I had the house — fine — as it is I have been left with an inheritance that can be nothing but a millstone around my neck. All the money has been syphoned off in bequests to all and sundry and the damn place is saddled with a monstrous mortgage. I have no alternative but to put it up for sale and if there is anything left at the end then I shall certainly consider myself fortunate indeed.'

'You are right there,' Tim told him bluntly. 'If you ask me you are a damn sight luckier than you deserve to be. Now, please leave Maggie alone — give her a chance to recover from your mother's totally unwarranted assault.'

'I am *not* asking you.' Nigel shot a look of concentrated malice at us both; 'As for leaving Maggie alone, that will give me the greatest pleasure. Naïve little girls from Down Under without even the wit to achieve what they obviously came to do are not my type.'

To my great relief he turned on his heel and walked, straight backed, across the room and out the door. I watched him go then to my horror I felt the hot tears of humiliation and pain running down my face. I wanted to hotly deny Nigel's insinuations instead of which I sat here weeping, just as I might have done if they had been true and I had, as he insinuated, failed in my mission.

Tim picked up the discarded brandy glass and passed it to me. 'Drink up!' he ordered. At the same time Sybil passed me a clean, white lace handkerchief.

'And mop up,' she instructed. Her voice

was dry but a small smile curved her lips. 'We don't, for one moment, believe Nigel's suggestions, do we?' She turned to Tim and I caught the ghost of a smile between them, this was the most comforting sight: if these two were my allies, I thought, I had nothing whatever to fear. Anyway, Nigel had left, so . . . I twisted my head round so that I could look up at them and managed a smile as I sniffed hard and did the best I could to mop up my tears. Tim indicated the brandy and made a drinking motion. Obediently I took another sip, or rather a gulp that made me choke. I put it down and managed a real smile this time. 'I think I have had enough,' I told him. 'I don't think I shall ever be a brandy drinker.'

'Tea — hot, strong and sweet, is what is called for now.' Great-Aunt Sybil's voice was firm, as was her hand under my elbow. 'Do you think you can make it up the stairs to my room, my dear?' When I nodded and with help from Tim struggled to my feet, she added, 'I have something I need to talk to you about.' She stopped for a moment in the hall, then turning to Tim she said, 'could you help Maggie up the stairs while I go and ask for tea?'

I was in two minds whether to be independent and shrug him off or play the helpless female and let him assist me up that long flight of stairs. The fact that my legs felt oddly shaky forced me to accept his help with as good a grace as possible. In point of fact I found the nearness of his body not only comforting but also very right. I leaned into him as we moved slowly upwards step by step.

'Some staircase this!' Tim sounded quite awestruck as we reached the top and he looked back the way we had come.

'Yes — it is,' I agreed. 'We certainly do not see many like this back home do we?' With my attention drawn to the staircase I remembered the difficulty Sybil had with it and how I had helped her myself on occasions. I had a sudden vision of her attempting the ascent with a loaded tea tray. 'I'm fine now,' I assured Tim as we reached the upper landing. 'But I'm worried about Sybil; it's not so long ago that she was completely confined to her room, so do you think you could go down and give her a hand now?'

'You are quite sure you are OK?' he asked anxiously. I nodded towards the closed door of my great-aunt's room. 'I'll go in and sit down to wait for her,' I told him, standing for a moment, my hand on the door knob, to watch him bound lightly down the stairs.

There was something about him that gave my spirits such an uplift that I waited there till I saw Great-Aunt Sybil returning from the kitchen, with, as I had feared, a small tray of tea things. With some relief I saw Tim take it from her to walk slowly by her side up the staircase. She had her left hand on the banister and moved from step to step with care. I noticed there were three cups on the tray. Once in her room, Sybil sat down with a sigh in her favourite chair and Tim without being instructed placed the tray down on the table at her side. She thanked him, then looked from me to Tim and back again before asking in her direct way, 'I take it that you don't mind this young man hearing what I have to say?'

I shook my head. I could not imagine that there was anything she could say that I could in any way object to him hearing, but I was somewhat embarrassed when she turned to Tim and asked, 'And you? What are your feelings for Maggie, are you just a casual friend or is there something more?'

He didn't answer for a moment, then looking at me but speaking to my aunt he said, 'I would like to think I am much more than a casual friend, but I have no idea how Maggie feels.'

I found myself blushing furiously and

somewhat ungraciously urged Sybil to say whatever she had to say for goodness sake, I didn't mind who heard it.

'You may not, but I may,' she chided me gently. 'For what I have to say is as much my concern as it is yours.'

I mumbled some sort of apology and accepted the cup of tea she offered me. In silence we all sipped the hot liquid. I was beginning to get impatient again and wonder what sort of charade this was when she finally replaced her cup in the saucer and looking from one to the other of us began to speak.

'First,' she said, 'I must tell you that your grandfather was not your grandfather.' With what seemed to me a fine sense of drama she paused after this extraordinary statement and looked from one to the other of us. I sat there with my teacup in mid air, halfway to my mouth wondering if I had heard correctly or was relapsing back into semi-consciousness.

'Wh-what do you mean?' I stammered foolishly. 'If grandfather was not actually my grandfather, then who am I?' It seemed to me that the only answer to the conundrum she had posed was that I simply was someone else.

Great-Aunt Sybil smiled. 'Relax, child, you don't have anything to worry about. You are still Maggie. The only change is in your grandparent. The man you thought was your grandfather was actually your great-uncle.'

I shook my head in an attempt to clarify my thoughts and understand what she was saying. Slowly I raised my cup to my lips and drank the strong sweet tea looking at her over the rim of my cup. 'Then who am I?'

Sybil smiled and putting down her cup leaned over towards me and dropped her hand lightly on my arm. 'You are exactly who you thought you were; well almost, true you haven't a grandfather but you do have a grandmother.'

'Who?' I demanded, the sudden fear that my mad Step-Aunt Natalie might turn out to be my grandmother sharpening my voice.

'Me — I am your grandmother, my dear.' she said softly, adding rather tremulously in response to my astonished exclamation. 'I do hope you don't mind?'

I shook my head, of course I didn't mind, quite the opposite. If I was going to suddenly discover I had a grandmother there was no one I would have liked better than my Great-Aunt Sybil. 'Then ..' I stammered 'you are . . . my mother was . . . your daughter?'

She nodded. 'Of course,' she said quietly.

Impulsively I put my cup down and crossed swiftly to her to plant a rather noisy kiss on her cheek. 'I'm glad — really glad that you are my grandmother!' I told her, my voice choked by the rush of emotion I felt at this discovery. As I would have moved back to my own chair she caught my hand in hers and kissed me back.

'Thank you!' she whispered before releasing me. I sank back into my own chair, gulped and picking up my teacup drained it. I still didn't understand.

'But . . . ' I stammered, throwing her a look of appeal and shrugging to express my total confusion. 'Don't go!' I said sharply to Tim who had got up and replaced his cup on the tray. Even with this new and for the most part comforting revelation, the thought of staying in this house any longer than necessary scared me.

'Don't worry, I'm not leaving — I'll be waiting for you downstairs.' He smiled reassuringly, and it was comforting to know that he guessed how I felt. 'But I think your — grandmother would prefer to tell you the story herself, after all it is her very personal story.'

I glanced across at my grandmother and knew by the way she relaxed and threw him a small grateful smile that he was right. 'I won't keep her long,' she told Tim. 'And then you can take her away.' She remained silent for so long that I wondered if she had changed her mind after all about explaining my ancestry to me. Finally, she looked directly at me but her smile was hesitant. 'I do hope you are not upset at finding I am your grandmother?'

I reached out impulsively and put my hand on her arm. 'Upset? Oh, No! I can't imagine anyone in the whole wide world I would rather have than you!'

'Oh, Maggie, do you really mean that? You make me so happy. Certainly for my part you are everything I could ever have hoped for in a granddaughter, just as your mother was everything I could have wanted in a daughter . . . ' Her voice trailed away and she fumbled for her handkerchief and dabbed her eyes. 'It was a great sorrow to me that she never knew our true relationship. I always planned to tell her when she was grown up, then she met your father and ran away to Australia with him.'

I already felt I knew the story from this point. 'Can you explain to me,' I asked softly, leaning towards her and resting my hand on her knee, 'why she never knew you were her mother?'

The old lady sighed. 'Oh, it's a simple enough story, and as old as time,' she said with some bitterness. 'I was young and foolish and I fell in love and got pregnant. When I told my lover he melted away like butter in the sun. I learned much later on that he already had a wife. I came to stay here with my brother and his wife, at my wit's end to know what to do. Sarah, my sister-in-law, was one of my oldest and best friends, we had been through school together, she guessed I was pregnant, at first she was quite distraught, really angry in fact. Then she told me the reason, she had just found out that she could never have a living child, she had already had a series of miscarriages. It was Sarah who came up with the solution to all our problems; we would let the world think the baby was hers. That way she would have the child she longed for and I would not be disgraced.' She paused and I could see her mind was taking her back in time. 'It is far easier to give away the baby inside you than the one in your arms,' she said sadly.

I patted her arm and made some sort of sympathetic noise and she continued. 'But I begged to be allowed to live here so that I could know my daughter and see her grow up. My brother only agreed on condition I was sworn to secrecy. Of course I agreed, and kept my word until this moment. It was hard, especially when Sarah died when your mother was only five years old, but I was grateful to be here and to be, as the world thought, a surrogate mother to her.'

'Why have you decided to tell me now?' I asked.

'I feel you have a right to know the truth, and as the man you thought was your grandfather is dead he cannot be hurt. I had, in fact begged him to tell you himself and I think he planned to do that; our longstanding quarrel was because I wanted your mother, and you, put in the picture. When he realized that you were in danger he said he would tell you. But as you know, he didn't get the chance.'

For a moment just whom I was related to didn't seem so important. 'Why did he think I was in danger?' I asked.

'Natalie was convinced you had come back to claim your inheritance. She thought she could persuade Nigel to woo and win you and get everything that way, when that didn't seem to be working she put plan B into operation — eliminate you, that is why my brother stipulated that you must return to Australia. I am afraid he didn't bargain for her going right off the handle and actually killing him.'

'But why — what could she possibly hope to gain with the cat fur parcels?' I asked, feeling for the first time a deep sympathy for the man I had believed to be my grandfather. Great-Aunt Sybil (I was finding it hard to think of her as anything else) shrugged.

'I think her hatred of George and myself coupled with her obsessive and possessive love for her son has totally deranged her.' She paused, looked at me and smiled, her words when she continued latched on to my thoughts. 'Don't worry, Maggie. She has no idea of your true identity and will not learn it through me.' She gave me a tremulous smile. 'All the same, my dear, I will feel a good deal happier when you have left this house, even though Natalie is, I hope, safely held by the law.'

I got up and hugged her. 'But what about you? I don't want to leave you, dear grandmother.'

For a fleeting moment she hugged me back, then pushing me away she said briskly. 'Go along with you — that nice young man is downstairs. Don't keep him waiting!'

16

There was no sign of Tim when I got down into the hall, I looked hastily into the rooms radiating out from the big hall, but he wasn't in any of them. I was quite sure he would not have left for London without me so took the opportunity to go down to the kitchen and say my farewells to the Ingrams. They, and my newly discovered grandmother, were among the few happy memories I would take away from this place.

I pushed open the door and there was Tim, seated opposite the old couple at the kitchen table, between them was the large brown teapot and a plate of Hilda's scones. God knows when she had found time to bake them, and Tim was drinking yet more tea. They all turned and smiled at me as I stepped into the kitchen, the one really friendly room in the house. Tim patted the chair at his side and Hilda jumped up to pour more hot water in the teapot. I shook my head but Tim insisted on, 'One for the road,' and when Hilda pushed the plate of scones towards me I took one realizing that I was actually quite hungry. I had been far too strung-up earlier to eat.

'Well?' Tim asked. I was tempted to retort with 'Well what?' Then remembering how all three of the people sitting at the table with me had been kind and supportive, I decided to tell them the truth. My grandmother, as I had to learn to think of her, had not sworn me to secrecy with them.

'So, she told you, did she?' was Hilda's disappointing comment. I had expected surprise if not astonishment at my revelation.

'You knew — all the time?'

Her husband smiled at me. 'We knew.'

'But . . . ' I stammered, not quite sure what I was actually going to say. Hilda reached across the table and squeezed my hand. 'I was with your grandmother when your mother was born,' she explained. 'That was why she was always so special to me.' Her voice broke and her eyes filled with tears and her husband took up the story.

'The master took a house in Cornwall for the whole summer and we all went down there, him and the mistress and Miss Sybil. When we came back here in the autumn no one questioned that the baby belonged to the master and mistress; everyone was happy, they had a child and your grandmother was spared what would have been a dreadful scandal and disgrace in those days.'

'And you and Hilda were sworn to secrecy?

The old man drew himself up and I realized I had hurt his pride. 'They knew we wouldn't gossip,' he said coldly.

I would have apologized if I had known what to say but Hilda beamed at me. 'Your mother was such a joy to everyone, we wouldn't have done a thing to hurt her. Then there was more trouble and she left.' Her expression clouded but cleared again when she added, 'Then you came and it was as if she herself had come home!'

There was one more thing I wanted to know before I left; most likely for ever.

'Why did my mother run away?' I asked.

'She never told you?' Hilda sounded astonished.

I shook my head. 'Please, will you tell me?' I begged.

'She fell in love with this young man, he came to photograph the horses for some reason or other, he was very attractive.' I got the impression she had been going to say something derogatory then remembered that it was my father she was speaking of. 'She fell quite head over heels in love with him, and he seemed attracted to her, anyway your aunt and your grandfather, that is your grandmother and your great-uncle, tried to make her wait. He was off on some trip to Australia and planned to come back in six months, they begged her to wait till then, but she was young, hot-headed, and I suppose we had all spoilt her. Anyway, she wouldn't listen, she went with him, just leaving a note to say what she had done. We all hoped that when the six months was up she would be back, for a while at any rate. But we never saw her again, nor heard, and in fact we didn't know what had happened till you turned up.'

Hilda looked pensive. 'I wish I had known about the letters,' she said with a sigh.

I nodded sagely. 'It didn't work out; my father left her when I was a very young baby. I suppose she was too proud to admit that she had been wrong. All the same, I can't understand her not writing, she loved you all so much it doesn't seem like her.'

'She did write.' Mr Ingram's words broke the silence. I looked at him in surprise and was about to ask how he knew when he added, 'Your grandfather, your great-uncle, intercepted the letters; he was so angry and upset by what he saw as your mother's defiance and anxious that his sister, your grandmother, should not be further upset he kept the letters from her. Just before he — died, he called me into his study and handed this packet of letters to me. When I looked puzzled he said they were old letters from your mother. 'Put them on the fire,

Ingram,' he ordered me, 'before they cause any more harm.' So I did, I did just that, I burned them on the Aga.'

'Oh!' I didn't know what to say, would it have made a difference if my grandmother had received them?

Hilda, dear kind Hilda, herself just as shattered as I, for her husband had not told her this before, leaned towards me. 'He must have wanted to make his peace with you, but then he was — killed, and it was too late.'

'Yes,' I said. 'Far too late.' What a sad epitaph I thought as I replaced my cup in the saucer and turned to Tim. I felt my heart miss a beat when he smiled into my eyes.

'Come along,' he urged, 'or we shall be far too late getting back into London.'

We do hope that you have enjoyed reading this large print book.

Did you know that all of our titles are available for purchase?

We publish a wide range of high quality large print books including:
Romances, Mysteries, Classics
General Fiction
Non Fiction and Westerns

Special interest titles available in large print are:
The Little Oxford Dictionary
Music Book
Song Book
Hymn Book
Service Book

Also available from us courtesy of Oxford University Press:
Young Readers' Dictionary
(large print edition)
Young Readers' Thesaurus
(large print edition)

For further information or a free brochure, please contact us at:
Ulverscroft Large Print Books Ltd.,
The Green, Bradgate Road, Anstey,
Leicester, LE7 7FU, England.
Tel: (00 44) 0116 236 4325
Fax: (00 44) 0116 234 0205

A PINCH OF SUGAR

Louise Pakeman

Eve has always tried to please the men in her life. Then an invitation to spend Christmas in Australia with Bill McMahon, a man she has been corresponding with over the Internet, tempts her to please herself for a change. But her holiday gets off to an unpromising start when she receives a frosty reception from Bill's daughter, Chloe, who knew nothing about her . . . As Eve and Bill struggle to communicate face to face, all appears lost. They must weather misunderstandings and a disagreement before Bill finally realizes what Eve means to him. But is he too late?

FLOWERS FOR THE JOURNEY

Louise Pakeman

Thirty, Clare reflects on her birthday, is a milestone in her life. Despite being a successful lawyer with a comfortable lifestyle in Melbourne, she feels that she's in a rut, particularly in her relationship with Robert. She wonders whether she wants to remain in it forever. And then a surprising letter amongst her birthday cards prompts Clare to take a holiday to meet the person who penned it, and a man and a dog with the power to change her life. With the security she has earned, dare she choose this alternative future?